A FAIR TRIAL

CALIFORNIA
LA LAW
The Golden State ™

A FAIR TRIAL

CHARLES BUTLER

Boxtree

First published in the UK 1991
by BOXTREE LIMITED, 36 Tavistock Street,
London WC2E 7PB

1 3 5 7 9 10 8 6 4 2

ISBN: 1 85283 606 7

Photoset by Rowland Phototypesetting Limited,
Bury St Edmunds, Suffolk

Printed and bound in Great Britain by Cox & Wyman Limited,
Reading, Berks.

A catalogue record for this book is available from the
British Library

Chapter One

It was a good day for Chuck Carlton. He had been woken in his Spanish-colonial style villa in the foothills above Malibu, by his girlfriend, Janice, calling from San Francisco where she had been attending a special course on psycho-therapy for the children of alcoholics. The course had finished a day earlier than scheduled, and she was flying into L.A. at lunchtime. She then reminded him that it was nearly a week since they'd made love – adding that for her that was too long. He heartily agreed, and made a mental note to cancel all his afternoon appointments.

But first there was another, perhaps even more exquisite pleasure awaiting him – at the downtown showrooms of Auto-Europa, on Wilshire. Here he took possession of a brand-new BMW convertible – smoky silver-grey with a black roof, dark grey upholstery and

1

the dashboard showing 500 miles on the clock, which meant the engine was run-in, and a maximum speed of 140 mph – nearly three times the legal limit in every state in the Union.

He signed all the papers and handed over, in part-exchange, his beat-up old Ford Mustang – a great car for pulling the girls at beach parties, but not quite the executive image needed for one of the most prestigious advertising agencies in California. He felt over ten feet tall and more than a million bucks as he signed the cheque, well into five figures – reflecting that his bank could well bear the strain.

As he strode out of the office, with the obsequious salesman padding at his heels, he caught sight of one of the secretaries watching him misty-eyed from behind her desk. Chuck Carlton returned the look, his eyes locking on to hers like the radar of some missile. He had always known, since high school, that he was highly attractive to women; he had those sort of looks that suggest the innocent high spirits of an overgrown schoolboy, combined with a well-muscled golden-haired hunk of beefcake with a reasonably-sized brain attached.

Carlton settled into the seat and tested all the controls, like a test-pilot before take-off. He loved cars, and an expensive new car revived in him all the thrills of opening presents as a child. But it was more than that. As he carefully nosed the car out on to Sunset Boulevard he experienced a sensuous delight, warm and glowing that was almost comparable to being with Janice – lifting her dress up over her waist and sliding his hand down under her tights, peeling them over her plump satin-smooth buttocks . . .

He slipped the manual gears into second and pulled away from a set of lights with a long low roar that he felt perfectly fitted his mood, both mental and physical.

Yes, it was a good day for Chuck Carlton – the 32-year-old account executive with Simbel Horne Inc. – soon, he had been assured only last week by Arthur Simbel himself, to become Simbel Horne and Carlton. Yep. Chuck was on his way – up and up. He had a beautiful home, a beautiful car, a beautiful girl, and a job with a beautiful salary that would soon be bringing in around a quarter of a million dollars a year.

As he glided along Wilshire, with the hood down, he could barely resist the urge to stand up in his seat and cheer at the sky. For today even the weather seemed to be in harmony with his mood. A stiff breeze off the ocean had scooped away the yellow smog, and in a rare moment of glory the sun burned down with diamond brilliance, etching out the endless stream of traffic and rows of white featureless buildings in what some wag had once called 'Seven Suburbs in Search of a City'.

But not only was his luck holding – it was getting better! An experienced gambler might have grown wary, knowing that all luck has to run out – sometimes with a vengeance. But Chuck Carlton was a born optimist. He seized his pleasures as they came, and could think of no reason why they should not go on coming until the grave. Not that he ever thought of the grave as such. Death, along with penury and terminal illness, were things that happened to other people. They just didn't happen to bright young executives driving a drop-head German car, to put in two hours at the office, before picking up the lovely Janice at the airport.

He put the BMW in the basement parking lot and rode up to the tenth floor where Marlene, the secretary on the front desk, smiled sweetly from under her long dark eyelashes. He smiled back, with that lethal look that said I'm tough and hard and amusing, and I'm damned good in bed, but sorry, kiddo. I'm already booked, from lunchtime on.

As he turned towards his office, she said, 'Oh, Mr Carlton, I have a message from Mr Simbel. He said he wants to see you as soon as you come in.'

Carlton frowned. The detour to collect the car had made him only thirty minutes late. He couldn't imagine old Simbel holding that against him. He fought the urge to light a cigarette, went along the corridor and knocked. 'Come in!' A thin man in a dark suit rose from behind a desk the size of a billiard table. 'Hi Chuck! Sit yourself down!'

Carlton waded across a deep white carpet that felt like soft snow under his feet and sat down in a black leather designer-chair that pitched him so far back that he had to grip the tubular arms for support. There was a rumour round the office that this was the Execution Chair which Old Man Simbel reserved for those he was about to fire. But Carlton felt only a very slight twinge of worry. This was his lucky day. And anyway, he was riding high – all set for a top place in the corporation, and the salary to go with it. In anticipation he flashed his even white smile.

Arthur Simbel responded with a long hard stare; then leant forward and opened a folder bound in dark red morocco. He studied it for several seconds. Carlton watched him, and for the first time began to feel uneasy.

Then Simbel smiled. 'Chuck, it pleases me to inform you that you have landed for us the Praxel account. Every clause okayed. No conditions, no strings. The whole shooting match!' He stood up, and Carlton struggled out of his chair, and the two shook hands across the expanse of desk. 'Well done, my boy! I thought we might celebrate with lunch at the Beau Sejour.'

Carlton hesitated. 'That's mighty kind of you, Arthur. Trouble is, I gotta meet someone in at the airport.'

'Oh.' Simbel gave a conspiratorial smile. 'Can I guess? That lovely young doctor from the children's hospital in Pasadena?'

'That's right. How did you guess?' Carlton frowned, mildly irritated that his boss should know so much about his personal affairs, as well as mindful of the need to avoid any hint of the sleaze-factor. For even here in L.A. – this latter-day breeze-block Babylon – the advertising house of Simbel Horne Inc. still managed to boast a reputation for professional integrity.

Simbel said, 'She called you here from San Francisco Airport. Just in case you couldn't make it.' He gave a dry chuckle. 'It's all right, my boy – I invited her too. Lunch for three – 2 pm at the Beau Sejour.'

Carlton nodded. 'Did you tell her what we're celebrating?'

'I just said it was a special occasion.'

Carlton swallowed hard. For a moment the awful thought struck him that she might be anticipating a proposal of marriage. And this was something that very much did not fit in with Chuck Carlton's idea of a lucky day. But so far, so good. Marriage could always wait for another day . . .

*

The Boeing 723 touched down just after 12.30. He was waiting for her at the gate. She was wearing a white linen suit that showed up the dark Titian red of her hair. He folded her to him, feeling her body envelope him, warm and alive; and she removed her glasses to let him kiss, long and lingering. Then she broke away, with a small teasing giggle. 'Hey wait a minute – it's only a week, Chuck! You behave like a guy just out of the penitentiary!'

'Too right!' he said, catching his breath. 'Right now I could eat you alive – every bit of you. Every tiny itsy-bitsy . . .'

'Well,' she said, breaking half free of him, 'it appears we'll have to make do with déjeuner à trois with your lord and master, Nice Old Uncle Arthur.'

'Uh-huh.' He led the way to the baggage conveyor, picking out her pair of pigskin cases that matched the vanity case she was carrying. 'Is he a Dutch uncle or a sugar-daddy?'

She put her head back and gave a small laugh, like the sound of a pure bell. 'He's just a nice old middle-aged man who has his employees' best interests at heart.'

'Meaning?' They were out of the terminal now, dodging the two lanes of traffic, making for the short-stay car park.

'Just like I said. He believes in steady relationships. Keeping his troops in line.'

'So he didn't give you the glad tidings?'

'No. What?'

'I got the Praxel account.'

'What! Oh Chuck that's wonderful!' She grabbed his arm and kissed him furiously on the mouth. 'Chuck, you're a lovely man and a genius!' He walked on between the rows of cars, basking in her excited admiration. When they reached the gleaming BMW she paused, then stared as Carlton stepped round and unlocked the passenger door for her. 'What happened to the Mustang?' she said.

'It retired. Old age.' He jumped in beside her and switched on the ignition. 'What do you think?'

She had her dark glasses back on and wrinkled her nose in mock disapproval. 'Well it doesn't have quite the same *je ne sais quoi* as the Mustang. But I'm sure it's a very good automobile.'

'The best.' Carlton swung the wheel and the fresh tyres squealed out of the car-lot gates, the powerful engine accelerating with a low smooth roar as they joined the freeway back into L.A. 'In fact,' he went on, determined to counter her habit of using French,

7

which always annoyed him because he never quite understood it. 'In fact, this engine which is now propelling us to the best restaurant on the West Coast, is the same make of engine – or an earlier version of it – which took the German Army into Poland and Russia.'

'I'm sure that information would go down dandy with your Jewish clients!'

He laughed, turning to watch her hair flowing out in the slip-stream like a mane of dark burning gold. And once again he felt a great surge of triumph, an urge to stand up in the driver's seat and yell that triumph at the steel-blue heavens. Nothing could stop him now. Not even slow him down. He was on his way to the top, with the sky the limit. Yessir! I'm Chuck Carlton who's just landed the Praxel account, and this is my girl who's a paediatrician with one of the City's biggest hospitals, and this is my brand-new car – and this surely is my lucky day.

Chapter Two

Luncheon didn't end until after three o'clock. This in itself indicated just how special the occasion was. Usually the staff of Simbel Horne Inc, from the chief executive officer downward, were permitted only forty-five minutes for lunch. Most made do with BLT sandwiches and coffee from the dispensing machines. And in accordance with the New Californian Morality, alcohol and smoking were strictly forbidden throughout the premises.

But today old Simbel waived the rules, which were of his making anyway. For the Praxel account was like being handed the crown jewels, and so deserved the very best. He duly ordered a bottle of Bordeaux '71. This was brought wrapped in a large folded napkin which the wine-waiter handled as though it were a new-born baby. Chuck Carlton accepted one glass,

9

which he drank warily, remembering his beautiful silvery-grey toy downstairs in the private car park.

Simbel's idea of conservation was to talk shop, and expect his guests to do likewise. He expanded, over the asparagus tips and wafer-thin Parma ham, about what Praxel would really mean to the corporation. Besides the aircraft and engineering side, there would be a network of contacts, layers of influence, coordinating political campaigns – mayors, judges, congress-men . . . ! He broke off, his flow of words staunched by a partially chewed piece of *gigot d'agneau*.

Carlton, perhaps because he was slightly in awe of his lord and master, nursed his single glass of wine and said little. He was mightily relieved when the coffee arrived and Simbel asked for a portable telephone on which he called up his stretch-limo – a Mercedes of grotesque proportions which Chuck Carlton had once likened to a German dentist's waiting room on wheels.

They both thanked him with genuine enthusiasm. The meal had been delicious and they were both begin-ning to feel drowsy. Simbel's bonhomie seemed to over-flow when they reached the glare of the street. 'You two kiddos'll want to be on your own I guess!' He slapped Carlton on the shoulder. 'Take the afternoon off, Chuck – this is VE Day!' And he gave Janice a chaste kiss on the cheek.

Carlton didn't bother to tell him that he'd already cancelled all his appointments for the rest of the day.

In the car he put his hand on her thigh, gently moving it up under her linen dress, feeling the edge of her French silk knickers, loose and smooth as quick-silver, and felt her whole body quiver; her head went back against the seat-rest and she gave a small moan. 'Oh Chuck! Chuck! Please, no, please. Please! Stop it, wait till we get to the house.

He gave a little proprietorial grin, removed his hand and switched on the ignition. 'Don't tell me that Old Man Simbel's turned you on?'

'Don't be silly. You think I really enjoyed listening to all that stuff about packaging senators for thirty-second sound-bytes?' She sounded a little out of breath and there was a high colour in her cheeks. For a few moments she remained with her head back, eyes closed.

Carlton chose the coast road along Santa Monica, past several miles of grey sand cluttered with what looked like glorified wooden shacks and beach huts, some of the larger ones fenced in behind razor-wire, and according to the realtor's guide, each dwelling costing at least one million dollars.

Although he'd had only the one glass of wine, Carlton began to feel drowsy too. The afternoon heat haze had joined with the clammy mist off the ocean, and it was only the slipstream of the open car that made the atmosphere tolerable.

Past Ocean Beach he turned on to the Santa Monica Freeway up towards Glendale and Pasadena. But the traffic was growing thicker, slower, till Carlton's beautiful machine was reduced to a sluggish 15 to 10 miles-per-hour; while the slipstream dropped, and the air outside grew hot and damp.

Carlton was becoming impatient, angry. He pulled

11

across into the inside lane, to a furious symphony of horns, and narrowly missed the front of a huge beer truck. Beside him Janice was gripping her knees, white-knuckled. 'Aw for God's sake, Chuck! Do you want us killed?'

'That's why I'm getting off at the next junction – make it through Beverly and West Hollywood.' She said nothing, sitting bolt upright, watching nervously for the next turning right. The sign said West Hollywood and Benedict Canyon. Quite a detour from his usual way home, but at least they were free of the traffic.

Janice began to relax, now they were off the freeway. Carlton smiled and patted her knee. Her only fault, he thought, was that she had never been a good front seat driver. Perhaps it had something to do with being a children's doctor, working in a hospital all day. At least, he, Chuck Carlton was insulated from most of the horrors of life . . .

The car was climbing steeply now, under tall heavy-scented eucalyptus trees which shaded them from the aching glare of the sun. It was cooler here, the houses were more solid, more spaced apart, the styles becoming more extravagant. American ranch-style, Tudor-ranch, executive Gothic-Tudor, Elizabethan English thatch, Spanish Colonial and French baroque, even a miniature castle out of the Brothers Grimm. All protected by private armed patrols, guard dogs, arc-lights and closed-circuitry concealed throughout the lawns and thick shrubbery. Carlton scented Old Money up here, or at least Old Hollywood, or what was left of it.

12

Some of these houses even looked as though they might last into the twenty-first century.

He hadn't been concentrating. Janice had dozed off, her hair secured under a Hermès scarf, while Chuck threw the powerful machine round the ever tightening bends and wondered about Mary Pickford and Fatty Arbuckle and the young Bogey. Soon he too – the young Charles Marcus Carlton – would join the Pantheon of the West Coast. Not with a name in lights, perhaps, but a power-broker – a master in the arts of publicity and communication: a man soon to have politicians, judges, even TV-moguls beating a path to his door. A Power Behind the Scenes.

He put his foot down, gathering speed as the road levelled out and began twisting now along the rim of the canyon. L.A. was far below – a great sprawling brown blur. And as he looked at it he realised that it was the wrong side. They were going in the wrong direction.

Janice had noticed it too. 'We better go back – take the San Diego Freeway to Bel Air.'

'That's miles back. As we're already here let's keep going. It's probably no further. If you can wait, that is?' he added, with a sly grin.

The road suddenly dipped into a long steep bend. Carlton had his foot down, watching her out of the corner of his eye.

'I dare say I can hold off,' she said, returning his grin; and her hand slid across his lap, hesitated, then leapt away like a frightened animal. And in the same moment she screamed, 'Chuck! Look out!'

He looked ahead and swung the wheel, but he was at least a second too late. Because of the steep incline and the drop into the canyon on his right, he had been tending to keep to the crown of the road. The car swung out of the bend below, and for a single, terrified second he saw it, bang in front of him, and saw the woman driver, her mouth opening in terror . . .

Janice began to scream too. He got his foot off the accelerator, groped for the brake-pedal, tried to swing the wheel inwards, and then waited for the crash.

Afterwards there was a great numbing silence. He thought he could hear dripping. Then the smell of petrol. He flung open his door and felt a stab of terrible pain in his right leg. 'Jan! Jan! Out! Out!' He was clambering round to the other side, growing sick with the pain, and aware now of another person screaming. Not Janice. She was already out of the BMW, her face white with horror, starting towards the other car. It was, or had been, a small two-door hatchback. The BMW had struck it head-on, and being the weaker car it had absorbed most of the impact. The engine-block had crumpled to a quarter its normal size and had finished up on the front seats. The woman driver was lying half upside down. She was wearing jeans, and her legs protruded at an odd angle, like a yoga position.

As Carlton peered in through the shattered windshield, he saw both legs give a sudden violent spasm, which was somehow far more horrible to him than the sight of blood.

Then he became aware again of the screaming. A thin agonised sound coming from somewhere under the

14

back seat. At first, through the mist of pain, he thought it was a dog. Janice had got there first and was now trying desperately to wrench open one of the doors. 'For Chrissake, Chuck, help me! There's a kid in there!'

Carlton struggled miserably round to her side, trying to lean all his weight on his good leg. And now came a low roaring sound in his ears that drowned out the wailing from the car. Then he heard Janice again. 'Help me, Chuck, help me!'

He was close enough to touch her now. He tried again, just one step, and the pain shot up through his leg, up his spine to explode somewhere at the back of his skill. Dimly he became aware of other people. People coming out of houses. Cars stopping. A woman shouted, 'I'll call an ambulance!'

Carlton slid down on to his knees and was sick.

Time passed. He had no idea how long. A small crowd had collected. There was arguing over what to do. Janice was telling them she was a doctor and that nothing must be done before the ambulance arrived. Carlton watched her long legs and her sweet buttocks under the white linen dress, as she tried to reach into the back of the little car. After what seemed a long time she straightened up, her face still white, and this time she was crying.

She didn't look at Carlton; didn't even seem to notice him. In fact, nobody seemed to be paying any attention to him at all. He was glad that Janice appeared unhurt, then thought miserably of his lovely new car, when he heard a man's voice on the edge of the crowd. 'That ambulance better be here pretty damn soon, or it'll be too late.'

'I think the driver's already gone,' said another, and began weeping.

'Someone better call the cops too!' the first man said. 'Just look at the position that bastard's car's in! Wrong goddam side o' the road!'

'And doing one helluva speed, I'd say. Just look at that engine!'

'Yeah. Head-on. The bastard!'

Carlton knelt against the crumpled side of the little car and listened to the voices which came from further and further away, and then to the sirens. Closer and closer.

Chapter Three

They lifted him into the second ambulance and gave him gas for the pain in his leg. It made him feel light-headed, even happy. He smiled across at Janice who was sitting on the other stretcher-bed, eyes closed, her hands clasped tightly in her lap. Probably in shock, he thought: Me, I'm the one who ought to be in shock! The medic gave him more gas and he smiled again.

'You the driver of the BMW out there?' It was a motorcycle patrolman with the smoked visor of his helmet pushed up, the face underneath half blanked out by large reflector glasses.

Carlton gave him a manly grin. 'I'm more than that, officer. I am actually the proud owner – was the proud owner of that fine machine out there.'

The patrolman was writing in a little book. Name: Charles Douglas Carlton. Address in Glendale.

Address and name of workplace. Details of driver's licence. Proof of identity and full particulars of driving insurance, medical insurance.

Carlton had them all to hand, in one large crocodile wallet. He grinned. 'What a drag, huh!' And he lowered his voice to a locker-room whisper. 'Was just on our way back to have a nice long screw –'

The face behind the mirrors nodded, tight-lipped. 'Under the laws of this State I am empowered to ask you to take the breathalyser test for possible alcohol . . .'

'Sure, officer!' He pulled himself up on one elbow, careful not to shift his bad leg.

The cop said, 'You know how to use this?'

'Sure, sure. I been around.' He breathed into the little tube, then settled back, smiling again. 'O.K., officer?'

The cop paused. 'Yeah. You're just within the limit.'

'I was a good boy, see. Just the one glass o' wine for lunch. Pity about the car, though. Very first day I have it – and *wham*!'

'If I was you, Mister Carlton, I'd be a lot more worried about the car you hit. And the people in it.' He slapped his notebook shut and turned with a creak of leather. 'This registers that you're under the limit *now*. It doesn't say what you were at the time o' the crash.'

'So what? I'm under the limit now. You just said so!'

'Yeah. Too bad. Because right now nothing would please me more than to bust you for the works. So long, pretty-boy. See you at the fatal accident inquiry.'

18

Carlton lay back on the mattress and stared at the roof of the ambulance. The engine started, they began to move. From outside came the crackle of police radios. 'I was under the legal limit,' he said. 'Under the legal limit.'

One of the medics leant out and felt his pulse. 'Sure you were. Just take it nice and easy now . . .'

*

Just two hours since the crash. Harsh white glare, Washington Hospital. Carlton and Janice were making for the main entrance. The hospital had lent him a stick; his leg had been X-rayed and found to be suffering from severe trauma but nothing was broken. Janice had no physical injuries, but was still in shock. Her eyes were fixed and glazed, and she had hardly spoken since leaving the ambulance.

Emergency was now crowded, but busy with the perpetual activity of a railway station or air terminal. Nobody was taking any notice of them. They were a few feet from the entrance when they both heard a loud angry shout from behind. It was a big man with thick grey hair and a face contorted with fury and grief. A nurse was beside him, nodding surreptitiously towards Carlton and Janice. At first Carlton, muzzy with painkillers, did not realise what was happening. Then the man came at them like a charging bull. They both stopped, staring.

'You murdering son of a bitch! You killed my wife! And my son's in there dying!' He had stopped barely a foot away from them, fists clenched, his whole body shaking as though a powerful electric current was passing through him. Carlton and Janice froze. Janice was the first to recover, despite her heavy sedation.

'It was an accident.'

'It was murder! This bastard –' His eyes were trained on Carlton like the twin barrels of a shotgun. '– My little son's back there in Intensive Care. He's lost half his blood. His face is all cut and bleeding –' He broke off with a sudden horrible grunt; his eyes exploded in tears.

Janice said gently, 'I'm really sorry. We both are. But he is in the best possible hands.'

He glared at them, uncomprehending. 'The police say you were on the wrong side of the road. And they said you'd been drinking.'

'I just had one glass of wine. I was within the limit.' As he spoke, he was aware that he should have kept silent – or at least have apologised, like Janice.

'You'd been drinking and you've killed my wife. And I'm telling you – if my little son dies I'm going to come after you and kill you.'

'It wasn't my fault. It was just an accident.' Again he thought, I must apologise. Say the right thing. But he was too late. A fist crashed into the side of his face and, combined with the effects of the pain-killers, he went down with a crash and lay still.

Suddenly, everyone in Emergency seemed to appear at once. The man was grabbed by an intern and a security guard. Janice seemed momentarily convulsed out of shock and, when Carlton came to, he was lying with his head cradled in her hands. The man was bawling obscenities while they dragged him away.

Carlton's face felt oddly numb and lopsided. He said, 'I'll get a lawyer – I'll sue you.'

'Yeah, you get a lawyer, Mister Carlton. You're sure going to need one.'

At that moment, a young man in a safari suit pushed through the crowd and took a photograph of Carlton on the floor and Janice still crouching by his side. He then took a photograph of the bereaved father, before Carlton could quite take in what was happening. But before the young man could ask him any questions, Carlton had made it through the Emergency doors, with Janice hurrying behind.

They were in time to catch a taxi which was just being vacated by an angry-looking woman and a man with a black eye.

*

The man in the safari suit stuck his card in the payphone and said, 'Sangster here. City desk.' Pause. 'Hello – Ed? Sangster, Washington Emergency. I got nothing on that drug death – at least, not yet. But I've got something else that might be interesting. A death crash up on Benedict. Woman killed and her five-year-old son on the critical list.' Another pause.

'Yeah, I know. There are hundreds of crashes every day in L.A. But the angle here is the other driver. The cop I talked to here says he was given the B-test and passed, but that he did admit to having had a drink. And the husband of the dead woman just walked up to our boy and knocked him out cold. Makes a really great pic.' He paused again. 'And the point is, I know this guy's face from somewhere. In fact, I think he's been through this before.'

Chapter Four

The taxi took two hours through the evening traffic to reach Carlton's house on Sepulveda. He and Janice had hardly exchanged more than a few words during the whole journey. She was half asleep most of the way, still muzzy from her sedation, while he now had two sources of physical pain – his traumatised leg, and his cheek and left eye which were swelling spectacularly. However, even more hurtful was the mental pain he was suffering: his ego was bruised as badly as his face and the memory of his crushed car caused him twinges of remorse.

Inside his house the red light was winking on his answerphone. Janice slumped into a corner of the long white chesterfield, and curled up her legs without kicking off her shoes. Carlton played back his messages: a couple from his secretary at the office confirming future appointments; one from a man who wanted to sell him a giraffe; and a final call, timed half an hour ago, from the administration officer at Washington Hospital. He said simply that the second crash victim, five-year-old Tommy McIvor, had just died. There was a click and a long dull whining sound.

Janice began to sob. Carlton went over to the horseshoe-shaped bar in the corner and poured himself a tumbler of neat Jack Daniels. The instructions on the painkillers in his pocket said 'NO DRIVING, NO ALCOHOL'. Well, driving was out for the moment, and to hell with the painkillers. They'd be all the more effective!

He had downed half the glass and was hobbling back to his leather Eames chair, when the telephone purred across the room. He heard Simbel's voice, quiet and suggestive. 'I hope I'm not disturbing you guys but I just thought I'd tell you that Praxel have laid on a whole weekend in Acapulco – Lear jet, the best hotel, the best of everything . . . Hello? Are you there, Chuck?'

Carlton sank on to his shaggy white sheepskin rug. He had to hold the phone with both hands. 'Sorry, sir. I just got in. We had a crash.'

'Are you hurt?'

'Not badly, though a guy in the hospital swung a haymaker at me and I'm not going to be very pretty in the morning.'

'Hit you? Who hit you? Why?'

'Seems I killed his wife and little boy. I drove my new car straight into them.'

'Oh God.' There was a long silence down the line.

Carlton took another slug of whisky. Then Simbel spoke again.

'Sounds like you're gonna need a lawyer, Chuck. A proper lawyer. The best. You take the day off tomorrow and leave it all to me.'

*

Carlton did not sleep well that night. Even after the whisky and painkillers, his mind refused to shut down. He had only to close his eyes, for his mind to start replaying every moment of the crash, in brilliant, horrible detail, so that he woke several times screaming and sobbing, his pyjamas dark with sweat.

Janice didn't come to him. She stayed sleeping on the chesterfield downstairs. And neither of them seemed to remember that they hadn't eaten. Just before midnight the phone rang. He cursed that he hadn't left the answering machine on. It went on ringing; stopped; started again. Who? he wondered. Simbel again? The hospital? The police?

He reached it at last. Breathing hard. Tongue furred. Left eye almost closed. And a steady thumping round the walls of his skull. '*Her-ler!*' He barely recognised the sound of his own voice.

'Mr Carlton? Mr Charles Carlton?'

'*Yer'her wann' him?*' His bruised face made it sound as though he were talking through a bag of pebbles.

'My name's Sangster. We met this evening. Briefly,

25

at the Washington Hospital. I'm with *The L.A. Clarion* and I'm calling just to check a few facts . . .'

Dimly, somewhere far back in his curdled brain, something told Carlton to hang up. Now! Pretend it was a wrong number, then switch on the machine and take no further calls. But the critical moment passed and he was still listening.

'. . . Like I said, I just wanna check a few facts. About the crash this afternoon up on Benedict Canyon. Did you know the kid died? Well, I been speakin' to his father – the guy who slugged you this evening at the hospital. He says he's going to kill you. And it seems the L.A.P.D. are taking it seriously. They been threatening to hold him in protective custody overnight. Seems he's an ex-Marine and has a gun which he knows how to use . . . Hello? Mr Carlton . . . ?'

'He's coming up here to kill me? He knows where I live?' It was as though Carlton were talking to himself.

'The L.A.P.D. was talking of sending up a patrol car to keep an eye on your place. Is it there yet?'

'Hang on.' Carlton crawled off the bed and looked out at the rows of parked cars, but none bore the insignia of the Los Angeles Police Department. Back at the 'phone he said, 'Nothing – yet. Do you think I should call the local cops?' And even as he spoke he wondered how it had come about that the great Chuck Carlton, soon to be of Simbel, Horne and Carlton, should be seeking advice at the dead of night from an intrusive hack whom he didn't even know.

Sangster went on, 'Just one other thing, Mr Carlton. Our records show that two years ago a certain Chuck

Carlton, then living on Venice Boulevard, was charged in the County of L.A. with drunk-driving. Am I on track?'

Carlton said nothing, his breathing shallow with the delayed pain of bruised ribs from the car's seat belt.

The reporter's voice droned on. 'It was the start of a big campaign against drinking and driving throughout the whole State. Judge Rosalind Acker led the field with a plea that the legal limit be abolished and that anyone convicted, with even a trace of alcohol in the blood, should be automatically banned from ever driving again. And in the event of someone being killed she was calling for a mandatory jail sentence of five years. Any of this familiar to you, Mr Carlton?'

Carlton was determined to keep what dignity he had left. 'Why not talk to the lady direct? I don't make the laws in this State.'

The voice chuckled down the line: 'You just could be wrong there, Mr Carlton. The lady judge is running for office in the Fall, and it's on a very tough law-and-order ticket. Which brings me to something else. Don't you work for the Simbel Horne Agency?'

Oh Christ! he thought. He knew he should say nothing more, deny everything, hang up on this little creep. Instead, he said, 'How the hell did you find that out?'

'Made a few calls, that's all. Sounds like you're a pretty bright boy. At least a couple of cuttings in our morgue say you're right on target for the top.'

Carlton suddenly felt a terrible bone-aching weariness flood over him. The telephone was slippery under

27

his fingers. 'Listen, asshole – just go play baseball in the traffic!'

There was a short cackle of laughter down the line. 'I like it. Pity I can't quote you. By the way, how's the eye?'

Carlton slammed the phone on to the floor, then doubled up and, with a massive, groping effort, just made it to the bathroom where he was violently sick.

Chapter Five

10.30 a.m. and the morning conference was well underway in the ninth-floor offices of the Los Angeles law firm of McKenzie Brackman. The first half-hour was taken up with various unfinished business.

'This whole race issue's getting like a virus,' McKenzie said, from his seat at the head of the table. 'Once it gets into the system, you just can't get rid of it!'

Brackman, the managing partner of the firm, sat across the table and his high bald dome nodded judiciously. 'Some of these people – and I mean lawyers as well as politicians – are getting to use the race angle like Senator Joe McCarthy used Communism. Throw it and it sticks. And goes on sticking.'

They all murmured their assent, except young Jonathan Rollins who stared in front of him, his dark face set grimly.

They were drafting a press statement on the Chisholm–Russ case, in order to combat an earlier statement by the plaintiffs accusing McKenzie Brackman of 'hidden racism'.

'Why don't we say,' suggested Michael Kuzak, 'that if the firm were racist – hidden or otherwise – we'd hardly be employing Jonathan at all, let alone have selected him to act as attorney for Brian Chisholm, who's white. In any case, Chisholm didn't complain once through the whole trial. It's only come up now.'

'How do you feel about that, Jonathan?'

Rollins looked relieved. 'I guess that'll do fine.'

'Moving along,' said Brackman. 'The Totten tax audit.' He turned his hard stare on Stuart Markowitz. 'How's it coming, Stuart?'

'It's not,' said Markowitz. 'I think I've persuaded the IRS to call off the dogs.'

'Wonderful,' Brackman said, and with his hard stare still measuring Markowitz, went on. 'And how are *you* feeling?'

Stuart Markowitz coloured with embarrassment and annoyance. It was less than two months since he'd had a coronary in the middle of a case – practically in the middle of the courtroom. And there was no way of scrubbing that from the record. He looked at Brackman and nodded. 'Fine!'

Brackman, with a small patronising smile, nodded back. 'Fine.'

Markowitz flushed even darker. 'I'm fine, Douglas. Just fine!'

Brackman nodded again, said 'Fine' again then let it

go. One thing he did not want was to have one of McKenzie Brackman's most loyal and long-serving employees sue the firm for unfair dismissal.

At that moment Leland McKenzie, the elder statesman, lifted his hand. 'All right, ladies and gentlemen . . . So what else have we got?'

Brackman glanced down at his notepad. 'Well . . . Lowens versus America's Most Embarrassing Practical Jokes.'

Across the table Victor Sifuentes looked glum. 'I just couldn't settle. Looks like it'll go to trial.'

'You gotta be kidding!' cried Arnie Becker. 'I mean, you don't think the guy's taking this a little too seriously?'

Brackman stared at him, grim and unblinking. 'The guy had his toupee lifted off on national television. How would you feel?'

Becker looked back at him, his jaw muscles working desperately to suppress the laugh that was very near the surface. 'Sorry, Doug. I can't relate. I mean, how would *you* feel?'

'I think he has a case,' Brackman said. 'These TV shows make millions in profits out of embarrassing people. Why not get them to share those profits with their victims?'

Leland McKenzie sat back in his chair. 'All right, are we done?'

'Just one more item,' said Brackman. 'Road accident – yesterday afternoon up on Benedict Canyon. Two dead – a mother and five-year-old son.'

'I saw it on the Breakfast News,' said Abby, her

delicate prettiness marred for a moment by the memory of the TV shots which had showed everything except the bodies. 'We'll be representing the father, I guess?'

'Well, erm . . .' Brackman groped for words, suddenly struck dumb.

Abby didn't help him by her next remark. 'In the TV item the police dropped a hint that the guy who was driving the other car had a drink-driving record. Pity the poor attorney who has to stand up in court and plead for him.'

There were strangled sounds coming from Brackman's end of the table. For once his usual air of ruthless efficiency was replaced by something approaching anguish.

Eventually, he regained control of himself. 'This is a priority case which we're handling for Simbel Horne. Arthur Simbel called me at home last night. The defendant is Charles Carlton, the agency's blue-eyed boy. Simbel is about to make him a partner. So there's obviously a lot at stake here. And the police had no business to give out information about Carlton.'

'It wasn't the police,' said Abby. 'They were interviewing the reporter who broke the story in the *L.A. Clarion*. I guess you didn't see it.'

'Not quite my style of morning reading,' commented Leland McKenzie drily. 'Anyway, let's decide who's to take this case before Joe Public decides whether the defendant's guilty or not guilty.' He turned to Ann Kelsey. 'Ann, how are you fixed?'

'Not me, Leland. I've got this Dairyland case coming up. My hands are full.'

32

'Yeah. Full of yoghurt!' Jonathan Rollins, relaxed now, smiled at her.

'What do you mean?' asked Sifuentes.

'Oh, you weren't here the day it was first discussed. Some guy is suing Dairyland because he claims he ate a tub of slug-flavoured yoghurt.'

Brackman could see that things were getting out of hand and tapped the table imperiously.

'Let's get back to the Carlton case. Kuzak, how about you?'

'I guess that's OK. I still have to tie up some loose ends on the Herbstman case, but that can wait.'

'OK then. To work, everybody!'

*

Carlton lit his fifth cigarette of the morning. He hadn't had one the whole week that Janice had been away but now his resolve had vanished. Every time he inhaled, his ribs hurt. He felt as though he had a giant hang-over but couldn't remember all that whisky on top of the painkillers. All he could remember was that one lousy glass of wine and his smashed sweetheart – his BMW. Did he love his car more than his fiancée? At that moment, yes.

'This is a no-smoking zone,' the blonde receptionist fluted. She spoke the way Barbie-Doll would if she could. Carlton looked around for an ashtray but, of course, there wasn't one. He dropped the cigarette into a vase of flowers and hoped the girl wouldn't notice. Otherwise she might accuse him of cruelty to roses. He looked at his watch. At last he was led into the attorney's office.

'Hi, I'm Michael Kuzak. Pleased to meet you!' Kuzak flashed his tough no-nonsense smile and waved Carlton to a chair.

Carlton reacted like a horse at too high a fence. In a city where good looks were hardly at a premium, he couldn't stand good looking men. He liked being the Adonis of every occasion; and, on this morning of all mornings, Kuzak's darkly handsome face set his teeth on edge and made his own swollen face ache even more. Nor was his mood improved by Kuzak's sympathetic grin.

'Boy, he must have slugged you one! Have you had a doctor look at it?'

'I don't need a doctor,' Carlton growled. 'I need a lawyer!'

Kuzak nodded. 'Well you got one. The question is, what can I best do for you?'

Carlton opened his briefcase and flung down that morning's copy of the *L.A. Clarion*. 'You read it?'

'Not if I can help it.'

Carlton pushed the folded paper across the coffee-table between them. Kuzak picked it up. He didn't have to look far. The words were splashed across the front page in letters two inches high:

YUPPIE ADMAN IN DEATH CRASH KILLS TWO.

And underneath, a fuzzed photograph of Carlton with tennis racket, smiling and showing his best Barrymore profile to the camera; and the further caption:

BACHELOR PLAYBOY IN DRINK-DRIVE SCANDAL.

This is not the first time that handsome, carefree Charles Carlton has been in trouble with the Law. Or with the Bottle . . .

Carlton watched keenly while Kuzak read. 'That other business – when I got stopped before – Christ, that was nearly four years ago. And anyway, nobody was hurt that time! I mean, can they print that kinda thing? Isn't it libellous? Can't I sue?'

'Well, the short answer to your first question is: Yes they can – and we've got the evidence right here to prove it. The answer to your other two questions is: Probably Yes – if you really want to go through with it, which you may well do now. But when you've had time to think it over, you'll most likely want to leave well alone. These papers make their money out of throwing shit at the fan. If you get them to publish an apology, nobody'll read it. In fact, most people who've read this stuff today will have forgotten who *the hell you are* by tomorrow!'

Carlton winced at such an easy trashing of his celebrity rating. He looked across the table at this dark, confident, handsome young man and said, 'How'd you like waking up and having something you did over three years ago splashed across half of Southern California? No way! You wouldn't like it one little bit!'

He got out his cigarettes, made a half gesture of offering one to Kuzak, who made a half gesture of declining, then sat back, crossed his legs, exhaled slowly, and said, 'I want you to get these bastards off my back!'

'The press, you mean?' Kuzak gave him a screwed-up grin. 'No way of doing that except by attracting more attention to yourself. Because technically what they've printed is not untrue. Although a sympathetic judge might rule in your favour – claiming the linkage of the drink-drive incident with yesterday's accident was activated by deliberate malice –'

'Which it damn well was!' roared Carlton.

'Okay. So it was malice. And let's suppose, when we've gone over all the problems, that we do sue for malice. Fine! In six months, a year, two years we get a judgement and a nice fat cheque to put in your bank, and everyone's happy. Everyone, that is, who's ever thought an unkind thought or said an unkind thing about Charles Carlton . . .' He spread his hands, palms up, and shook his head.

'So what the hell *do* I do?' cried Carlton, even more conscious that a man with a swollen cheek and blackened eye cannot become angry with dignity.

'Strictly speaking,' said Kuzak, 'my job as your attorney – *if* you agree to my representing you – is act on your instructions. Obviously, if I considered your instructions to be unreasonable, or not in your best interests – from whatever point of view – then I would counsel you as such.'

36

Carlton listened to him impatiently, and before Kuzak had finished was tugging out another cigarette and lighting it, keeping the smoke away from his bad eye. 'O.K. So on the strength of what Mr Simbel said, and what you see there in the paper, what do you counsel?'

There was a slight edge of sarcasm in his voice which Kuzak preferred to ignore. 'For a start, I strongly caution you against trying to tangle with the press – most particularly, the *Clarion*.'

'You want me to take it lying down? That it?'

'If you like – though it's not quite the way I'd put it.'

'So how the hell *would* you put it, Mr Kossak? – or whatever you call yourself!'

Kuzak levelled him with his best courtroom stare. 'I'll give it to you straight. Last night your boss, Mr Simbel, called up Douglas Brackman, who's senior executive partner here, and asked us to get you off the hook. "You" meaning the prestigious advertising agency of Simbel Horne Inc. Brackman, being a busy man, delegated the case to me. Okay so far?'

Chuck Carlton closed his bad eye and scowled out of his good one. 'You haven't mentioned the assault.'

'Well, I was coming to that. Trouble is, Mr Carlton –' he paused – 'How'd you like me to call you?'

Carlton shrugged. 'Please yourself.' His last cigarette had started his eye watering again.

'Trouble is, Mr Carlton, it's not just your ass we're covering. It's the firm of Simbel and Horne's ass. Meaning you go down – they go down. *Capisce?*'

'Go down?' Carlton left the words drifting in mid-air, like his cigarette smoke.

'To be blunt – publicity like that' – he nodded at the folded newspaper – 'could be the kiss of death for an ad agency like yours.'

'But hell, that was *three years ago*! And I wasn't with Simbel Horne then.' He paused, hand outstretched, his good eye pleading.

Kuzak nodded coldly. 'Sure you weren't then, but you are now.'

'But I wasn't drink-driving yesterday!'

'No, you weren't. But yesterday your car killed a young woman and her little boy. And to be quite frank' – he nodded again, grimly down at the newspaper – 'that's what scientists call a critical mass. Because in California right now drink-driving is rated about equal with hunting baby whales with an assault-rifle.'

Carlton suddenly slumped in his chair, his mouth slack with exhaustion and despair. 'Please God, what do I do?'

Chapter Six

All that morning the telephones had been purring in the palatial offices – known modestly as the Palazzo Belvedere – where the Reverend Alan Weekes held court daily among the lush pastures of Bel Air.

This morning one of his earliest callers was Judge Rosalind Acker, who acted as heart and lungs for a plethora of Californian pressure groups, including Women Against Rape (WAR), Women Against Violence Against Women (WAVAW), and Women Against Drink-Driving (WADD). Today she was wearing the cap of WADD, for her morning telephone call to the Rev. Weekes. To be able to speak direct to the great man was never easy, as his calls were filtered through at least two lines of secretaries, to sift out the cranks, the hoaxers, the unbalanced and the abusive.

But the name, Roz Acker, was programmed to be near the top of the list.

He came on the line, his honeyed tones lingering over each word. 'Roz baby! And how *a-a-a-a-are* you today?'

'Just fine, Reverend. All the better for hearing your voice. Have you seen the *Clarion* today?'

'Well no, I haven't, Roz. I find it a distasteful publication. But no doubt one of my staff will have it – for the record, you understand. We have to know our enemy in order to defeat him.'

'Yeah, well this one is for WADD. And I'll be highlighting it, of course, for the election campaign.'

The Reverend Weekes adjusted his bathrobe – he was always a late riser – and sipped his freshly-squeezed orange juice. 'What are the facts, Roz?'

He lay stretched out on the wine-red satin Recamier sofa and listened. He was a very large man and, while not exactly fat, he gave the impression of being made of some kind of composite rubber or pink plastic. He also seemed to have no hair – just a few tufts of pale fur above his ears – and his moon-shaped face was so smooth, it looked as though it had never been touched by a razor.

He let the woman do most of the talking. In any case, Roz Acker was not someone to be easily interrupted. She had a rasping metallic voice that seemed to grow louder the longer one listened. The Rev. Weekes had to hold the phone several inches away from his head.

'Roz, baby, you're wonderful!' When talking to those he knew well – those he jokingly referred to as *my*

40

fellow-conspirators – his voice lapsed into a pseudo-Cockney drawl, a mixture of Cary Grant and Alfred Hitchcock. In fact, this was not quite so inappropriate: for Alan Weekes had been born and brought up in Broadstairs, Kent, and had only come to America in his teens. He'd settled in California where he found work as a make-up specialist with one of the big studios, before launching himself into a career of Born-Again Evangelist and Fearless Crusader for Mr Average America against the relentless onslaught of Violence, Drink, Drugs, Divorce, Perverted Sex and Pornography.

Alan Weekes knew that he was far from the first to exploit such a moral seam, or that his approach was in any way original; but he also knew that it was a seam that ran very deep, right into the heart of perhaps one in every three American families. When asked – usually on TV – what was the driving force behind his mission, he replied that he was a mere Humble Messenger for the Higher Power – a spiritual super-salesman, a retailer in moral values. And, on the surface at least, his character appeared blameless: unmarried, a teetotaler, non-smoker and vegetarian.

'Roz baby, this is wonderful!' he cried, when the rasping voice down the phone had finally run its course. 'Of course, I'll be there! Just one proviso. I think it would be wise not to share the same platform. Not to make it too *obvious*, I mean. Fine! Just dandy . . . ! And oh, Roz, what did you say that reporter's name was from the *Clarion*? Sangster – fine!' He leaned out and scribbled a note with a tiny gold propelling pencil.

'You get your people out – WPBX and all the local networks – and I'll get straight on to the Evangelicals – cable and coast-to-coast.' He chuckled. 'By the weekend we'll have that glamour-boy frying in his own fat!'

*

'Kuzak! Michael Kuzak! Yeah, of course I'm a client. I was in his office just an hour ago!'

Chuck Carlton was shaking so much that he felt as though he might be going down with a fever. He was standing in the hallway, pressing himself against the inside wall so that the crowd outside could not see him. Christ! he thought, I'm a bloody prisoner in my own house!

He grabbed the phone more tightly, trying to steady his breathing. 'Mike Kuzak?'

'Speaking.' The voice was low and neutral. Carlton hadn't been making friends that morning.

'Mike – this is Carlton. I'm home. Yeah alone, except for about a hundred people outside, and two TV trucks blocking my driveway, and every sort of freak and odd-ball that's unemployed standing around giving instant sound-bytes on the virtues of locking up drunk-drivers and people who kill –' He broke off, literally choking on his own rage. 'For Chrissake, Kuzak, I wasn't drunk! One lousy glass of wine, I had! Who are all these people? Where are my Constitutional rights?!'

'Chuck – just hang in there. Don't answer the door or the phone. I'm on my way.'

'Hey – how do I know it's you?'

'I'll come wearing a sequined tiara and carrying a tennis racket.'

Carlton replaced the receiver, then crawled into the main room and reached the cords of the Venetian blinds without being seen. He repeated the operation in the kitchen and dining room. He then mixed himself a very strong drink, which he emptied in two long draughts; then refilled the glass, lit another cigarette, and crept upstairs to the bathroom.

He stared into the mirror and groaned. He looked appalling – even worse than when he'd shaved that morning. His pallor exaggerated the swollen cheek, which now had the appearance and texture of an over-ripe plum; while his damaged eye was completely closed, with a fleck of suppurating scum at the corner. God, I look like some vagrant! he thought. What will they think at Simbel Horne? Nice of old Simbel to have had my interests at heart – putting me in touch with McKenzie Brackman. It was quite another thing turning on your TV to get the evening news and have the livid, lopsided features of the Maniac Driver of Santa Monica staring out at you in your own sitting room . . .

He was close to tears – not for the first time on this dreadful day – as he leaned down and splashed cold water on to his face and neck, thinking, I'm already behaving like a goddam victim! I'm not a goddam victim! It was an accident. I'll show them. This is a free country, and an automobile is as much the right of the

Modern American as the horse was to his forebears one hundred years ago . . . I'm going to show the bastards! he thought, as he dabbed a moist flannel on to his closed eye.

But first he had another drink, fifty-fifty this time, with not much ice. He calculated that with half downtown L.A. making for all the best restaurants and watering-holes, it would take Michael Kuzak anything up to an hour to reach Carlton.

At intervals the doorbell buzzed; there'd be a very short pause, then a note would be pushed under the door. When these had accumulated to a handful, he crept down on all fours and read them. They seemed literate: *If you're looking for legal expenses the Globe and Sun will pay $20,000 advance. Exclusive, of course.* Or another, in a rather elegant female hand: *Do you sincerely feel that there are elements in City Hall who want to make capital out of this dreadful and painful accident?*

He remembered that *in extremis* a man will grasp at any straw, even a grubby note stuffed under his door by a pack of scribbling literary jackals who want nothing better than to build him up, then knock him down – the greater the height, the harder the fall. But that bright attorney, Michael Kuzak, had been retained by Simbel, and Kuzak had said sit tight, don't answer the phone, above all, don't answer the door.

Carlton stayed upstairs, keeping a watching brief on the crowd on the pavements. It had swelled considerably, and there was at least one extra camera team with full recording equipment. He wondered if they expected him to throw open the french windows in the bedroom and advance triumphantly on to the balcony, where he would deliver a ringing declamation on the Rights of the Common Man – Joe Soap – no-one so high nor so low – a Californian's home was his hacienda, his armed stockade, his Alamo . . .

More than thirty minutes had passed since he'd called Kuzak. Once again he ventured downstairs, treating any uncovered window as providing a clear sniper's shot from a telescopic zoom lens.

In a morbid, desperate way he was almost beginning to enjoy himself – if only as a way of distracting himself from the more awesome trials ahead. The Fatal Accident Inquiry. Then maybe an action for damages. In this State, getting involved with the law was like playing with an octopus in a swimming pool.

Against his better judgement he poured himself another whisky – a third of the bottle gone – but what the hell! he wouldn't be driving anywhere today. *Perhaps ever again* if that grandstanding bitch Roz Acker got herself elected – banning any driver with drink in his blood from ever driving again. And a driver who killed, with or without alcohol in the blood, would be automatically charged with Murder Two, minimum five years . . .

It was delayed shock, he thought. Skulking in one's own home like a fugitive, too scared to pass a window without being seen. *Death-Driver Carlton* – with glass in hand and a black eye . . . God, what would Janice's people think? Even worse, what would her employers think at the children's clinic where she worked in

Pasadena? It was a very exclusive place – the sort of place where the slightest whiff of scandal could lead to prompt dismissal. It was all in the small print – something about *relationships unbecoming to the good standing of the establishment* . . . And with the second drink inside him he envisaged even more terrible headlines:

WOMAN PAEDIATRICIAN LOVES CHILD MURDERER

Suddenly he became aware of a clamour outside, raised voices, shouts, a clatter of running feet. Stealthily, he took up his position beside the little window in the hallway near the kitchen; tweaked down the Venetian blind, and to his amazement he saw the bulk of the press corps decamping *en masse* down the street, with the TV mobile units lumbering along behind. Then, to his even greater astonishment, he saw Kuzak sprint through the gate and up the garden path of crazy-paving.

Carlton was close enough to open the door to him before he'd even rung. 'What the hell . . . ?'

'Right – lock up. Then stay close to me – head down, don't run, easy does it. My car's the white Porsche. It's unlocked. Get in – *don't look round*!'

The keys were in the ignition. Kuzak was in the driving seat before Carlton had time to close his door and strap himself in. The engine was a deep, satisfying roar from behind; and for a moment Carlton thought again of his beautiful BMW. It was a real bereavement.

He looked around once, and saw the ragged troupe of pressmen and their acolytes regrouping about five hundred yards down the road. Then Kuzak swung the wheel and they shrieked round a corner and were in the clear.

'*What the hell!*' Carlton said again. 'How did you get rid of them?'

For the next few seconds Kuzak concentrated on the road, keeping his speed well above the limit, taking a couple of lefts, then doubling back and doing a fast right to join the Pasadena Freeway north. Only then did he begin to relax, allowing his speed to drop to around the 55-mark.

'I guess we had about a hundred seconds' lead on them. They'll go crazy when they find out. But I'm betting on them heading west to Santa Monica.'

'But how did you get rid of them?'

'Aw, an old trick. Learnt it at law school. You get a pack of newsmen all hungry for the same story – you divert them.'

'But how?'

'Give them the chance of an even better story. Several of those boys know me. So as a lawyer I dropped the word that General Noriega is enjoying a two-day furlough with a woman friend at Number 1078 . . .'

'But that's old Matthew Horniman's place!'

'It sure is. As a former D.A. with a track record that makes Jesse Jackson look almost reactionary – well, who else would you expect to find playing host to one of the most illustrious members of the oppressed classes!'

Carlton nodded, taking his time lighting a cigarette, then offered one to Kuzak as an afterthought.

'Thanks, no. I want a quick death.'

'You are kidding, aren't you,' Carlton said at last. 'I mean, is the General really shacked up at Horniman's place?'

'Ah, now there is the beauty of it all! Because it's such a darn good story, no responsible newsman would dare pass it up.'

'They'll be back though,' Carlton said gloomily, 'and with a vengeance!'

'They'll be back, but you won't. You can stay at my place tonight – strict bachelor quarters – unless we can find somewhere to hide you out of town. What about your girlfriend?'

'She's pretty cut up. I think she'd like to spend a bit of time on her own. What about my job? I've just landed the Praxel account for Simbel Horne; that means the real big time. I can't just go AWOL at a time like this!'

Kuzak leaned both hands on the wheel, watching the road as he spoke. 'As I tried to explain earlier, Mr Carlton, you are not strictly my client. I have been retained by your employer, Mr Simbel. And not to mince words, his instructions to me are to protect, at all costs, the good name of Simbel Horne. In short, he doesn't want a lot of nasty headlines about one of his employees.'

'I'm practically a partner,' Carlton said indignantly.

'Sure. But not yet.'

'Simbel's a very decent man – always been very fair.'

'I'm sure he has. He also has a multi-million dollar business at stake.' Kuzak could sense the tension beside him – the anguished efforts by which Carlton tried to convince himself that Simbel had retained Kuzak as an act of loyalty to a colleague in trouble. The thought that Carlton might suddenly become expendable – an embarrassment to be disposed of without fuss or publicity – came to him as a horrible surprise. *Not me!* he thought. *They wouldn't do this to me!*

'If Simbel Horne try to get rid of me, will I have a case against them?'

'That's looking a little on the dark side, isn't it?'

'You tell me. You're the lawyer.'

'I'd say you got a more immediate problem. Like a certain Mr Colin McIvor.'

'*Who?*'

'Husband and father of the two who died in the crash.'

'The one who assaulted me in the hospital? Can I sue him?'

Kuzak took a deep breath, as he negotiated the turn down into Inglewood. 'If you want the publicity, sure. But you have one big problem first.'

'He's going to sue me? Well let him!'

'I'm afraid he's got something rather more serious in mind.'

'What?'

'He wants to kill you.'

Chapter Seven

Dr Janice Rhodes eased her aching body into an arm-chair. The staff day-room of the San Fernando Clinic for Children, Pasadena, happened to be empty at that moment and she allowed herself to give into her pain. Bruised ribs – what a trivial complaint. She felt guilty to be alive when the little boy and his mother were dead.

Over and over again, she replayed the accident in her mind like a film: the two cars approaching each other, sometimes at terrific speed and sometimes in slow motion. Her mental picture of what happened next varied. At the moment of impact she had been so sure she was dead that opening her eyes and seeing the world moving around her seemed unreal. Then the awful sound of the child from the other car. It was like no sound she had ever heard before – or, she fervently prayed, was ever likely to hear again.

The door swung open. One of the interns, Patricia Simpson – a young, rather boot-faced girl – came in and switched on the TV set on the wall, then sprawled out in the chair next to Janice. 'What a dog of a day! You know what I spent most of last night doing? *Baby-sitting for my ex-husband's girlfriend and their new kid aged two!*'

Janice was only half-listening. The TV screen was showing the midday news. The Gulf. White House. Some politician in a European capital. Then a break for commercials. Patricia Simpson was saying, 'Honest, Jan, you think I'm a sucker? I mean, he just called up at eight – *at eight, my ass!* – and said he was desperate, someone had let him down at the last moment . . .'

Janice was not listening at all now. She was sitting upright as though a bolt of electricity had passed through her. Her face was ashen, her eyes wide and staring.

On the TV screen was a close-up of two cars hideously entangled – one, a big silver brute, looked as though it were devouring the other which was barely recognisable as a car.

Janice let out a thin scream and put her face in her hands. Patricia said, 'Hey, Janice, are you okay? You look sick, kid. I'll get someone . . .'

Janice's hands still blocked out the nightmare images across the room, but the sound still reached her: a fruity bass voice, perfectly pitched to squeeze every drop of pathos and outrage it could from the few sentences available.

'*It happens every day, in every big city, every small*

51

*town, on every highway, every dirt-track in the country.
And when it happens what do we call it? We call it an
accident. Sure! A life here, a life there – what the hell.
It's an accident . . . !'*

Janice's eyes were drawn, mesmerized, to the large
round pale face on the little screen, his lips moist with
passion . . .

*'Just a little boy of five – it could be any little boy –
could be your little boy . . .'*

Now – horror of horrors – there was the front of
Chuck's house. And now – oh God no! – a full-face
mug-shot of him: the same as had appeared in this
morning's *Clarion*, taken yesterday evening in the hospital just after he'd been punched by the bereaved
father. Taken in a bad light, Chuck's noble profile was
blurred, his expression angry and scowling . . .

The face stayed on the screen for only a few seconds,
but to Janice it seemed an eternity. And he looked so
awful! He looked like a *thug*! The only consolation was
that the picture was so bad, perhaps no-one would
recognise him.

There was a woman on the screen now, dark and
tight-lipped, button-black eyes like raisins. '. . . *and we
know that in this case, as in so many others, the driver
was tested for alcohol – and tested positive – but as he
was just under the legal limit, he was allowed to walk
free. Which is more than can be said for Mrs McIvor
and her little Tommy. And if he's somewhere out there
– maybe watching this very programme – I'd just like to
say, how does it feel being a child murderer?'*

Janice burst into tears. Patricia came over and put

an arm round her shoulder. 'I'll be okay!' Janice sobbed. 'I've been overworking, that's all . . .'

The woman on the TV drilled on. '*Watch my lips –* *WADD – WOMEN AGAINST DRUNK-DRIVERS.*'

Patricia switched off the set and said, 'I'll get Dr Peters – I don't think you should do any more work today.'

Janice slumped back in her chair and her whole body was suddenly racked with an uncontrollable shaking and sobbing.

*

The Civil Court, in the County of Brentwood, Los Angeles, came to order with the appropriate degree of formal dignity. This was not the place for meting out crude justice to the criminal, the psychopath, the wicked and the insane. This was an altogether more decorous place. Here they traded in money and reputations – writs and claims and counter-claims; reputations made and broken; fortunes grabbed, or thrown wantonly away. And throughout, the lawyers looked calm and well-fed, and generally, pretty pleased with themselves.

Judge Steven Lang was in the chair, a mild and conscientious man with a reputation for being fair. Victor Sifuentes had his client on the stand – a university egghead called Martin Lowens – a bookish-looking man in his early forties, entirely unremarkable in appearance except for a large, very obvious wig.

Sifuentes had already rehearsed this moment. During the past few nights he'd even woken up sweating about it. *How was he going to keep a straight face throughout this?* He had composed his saturnine good looks into their most predatory expression, his dark eyes hooded, his body bent slightly forward like a cat about to spring.

'Mr Lowens, will you tell us how this tape came to be made?'

Lowens cleared his throat. Otherwise, he seemed perfectly at ease. 'Well, I *thought* I was taping a rebuttal to a TV news editorial. I'm a professor of Soviet history at UCLA, and they wanted my views on how *perestroika* has affected the average Soviet citizen – the man in the street, so to speak. At the time I thought the whole thing was legitimate.'

Sifuentes put his hand up to his jaw – in a purely precautionary gesture. 'And, sir – when did you first discover – er – that your hair had parted from your head?'

'When I saw it on television – along with about 20 million other people.'

Sifuentes nodded gravely. 'The defendants never told you they were going to air this?'

'Well yes' – Professor Lowens hesitated – 'but I didn't know what had actually happened to me until I saw the tape.'

Again Sifuentes nodded, with all the gravity he could manage. 'And Professor . . . I know this is difficult . . . but could you tell the court in your own words what it was like to see yourself become bald on national television?'

'Yes, sir. I'll try. But I can't really describe the humiliation. I've been held up to the most dreadful ridicule. Half my students seem to have seen it. And I'm snickered at by all my friends. I even lost my job.' Nervously, he put his hand up to the toupee and patted it.

'You lost your job because of this?' Sifuentes repeated.

'Yes. The dean told me he couldn't have a professor whom the students couldn't take seriously. So he fired me.'

'And have you been able to find other employment, sir?'

'Well,' said Lowens, 'after a couple of months I got another teaching job. But with a reduced salary and virtually no shot at tenure. I tell you, this thing has just devastated me.'

Sifuentes nodded and bowed slightly. He felt as though he'd just scaled a precipice. 'Thank you, Professor Lowens. I have nothing further.'

A stout young man with a moustache was on his feet, facing the stand. 'Let me get this quite clear, Professor. You gave my clients a signed release, authorising them to air the tape – did you not?'

'Well yes. But I never knew my toupee had been dislodged when I signed that release.'

The stout young lawyer rocked back on his heels, smiling sceptically. 'Aw now come on, Professor Lowens! You telling us that they yanked your rug off your head and you had no idea!'

The last words were drowned, as Sifuentes sprang to his feet: 'Objection to the term "rug".'

But the professor seemed unperturbed. 'I didn't realise. They'd stuck an earpiece in me, and a microphone on me. There were so many wires. I just didn't feel the fishing hooks on the hairpiece.'

The stout young lawyer ploughed on. 'But when they lifted it off? How could you not feel *that*?'

Professor Lowens smiled, as though to say, I really am doing my best . . . 'Well, I *did* feel something draughty, but when I put my hand up there, everything seemed okay. I thought the wires had just moved it a little.'

At this point Judge Lang intervened, his voice registering a mixture of curiosity and disbelief: 'Don't you glue it on?'

Lowens looked up at him, his face a study of injured innocence. 'I didn't use the glue that day because I knew I'd be under hot lights. The heat can sometimes make it go all gooey – plus when I sweat, the wool smells.'

The judge stared at him. 'I see.'

The stout lawyer was on his feet. 'Objection to the smell of the wool.'

The judge ignored him, and the professor went on: 'I was just so nervous and distracted, I didn't feel it happen.' He patted the toupee again, shifting it slightly over his left ear.

The judge nodded, then seemed to make up his mind. 'All right. Now look – I don't know how far this joke went or how humiliating it was. I want to see the tape.'

At this moment the dignity of the court collapsed,

like a dam breaking, and laughter flooded down from the gallery and swept over the rows of lawyers and jury, even for a fleeting second, the judge himself.

Only Professor Lowens seemed unable to share the joke. 'Oh my God,' he said feebly.

Judge Lang had gathered back his dignity and said, 'We're gonna set up some video monitors in here and look at this tomorrow, so we can all see for ourselves.'

Sifuentes stood up: 'Your Honour, my client would ask that the courtroom be sealed.'

'I think not,' the judge said dismissively. 'We should be able to take it. The day after tomorrow at two o'clock. We're adjourned.'

He hurried out of the courtroom, cheeks sucked in and shoulders heaving. Lowens sank down into his chair, his head in his hands. The toupee slipped perilously forward.

Sifuentes stood up: 'Your Honour, my client would judge out of the room before he started to howl with laughter, and his genuine pity for his bewildered client.

His professional integrity won. Approaching the professor, he said sympathetically, 'Sometimes a person's wish to defend his honour can turn against him.'

Chapter Eight

When the Reverend Alan Weekes emerged from his private quarters into the public reception room, he was dressed in all the majesty of his office – an office registered at Nr. 2884 Sunset Boulevard, Los Angeles, as 'The Heavenly Word Inc.', – with subsidiary offices in the Cayman Islands; Asuncion, Paraguay; and Lucerne, Switzerland.

Today he wore a silk magenta roll-neck sweater, of the kind made popular two decades earlier by Robert Kennedy; a maroon velvet jacket and tight midnight-blue trousers, sculpted over his ample hips and corseted at the waist by a cummerbund of broad white slub-silk; and on his tiny feet were white doe-skin moccasins over scarlet socks, which had prompted both his friends and foes to call him 'The Cardinal'.

He advanced soundlessly across the carpeted reception room, his huge hairless face wreathed in a wide beaming smile that enveloped his enormous face, like a child's drawing of the Man in the Moon. 'Roz baby! How lovely, how perfectly *gorgeous*!'

Roz Acker was sitting on a very uncomfortable Regency chair – one of a set donated to the Rev. Weekes by a grateful antique dealer in New Orleans who, on being told he was dying of AIDS, had bequeathed all his earthly goods to a variety of religious institutions, from the Catholic Church to the Mormons, the Moral Majority and the Episcopalians, right down to one-man bands like 'The Heavenly Word'. Such gestures appealed not only to Weekes' vanity and greed, but also to his sense of humour – like some insurance policy for getting into the Next World.

'Good afternoon, Alan. I'm glad you were able to find time to see me.'

'But dearest Madam, I am *always* able to find time for you!'

'That's not the impression I got from your secretary.' Roz Acker's mouth shut like a trap.

For a moment Weekes leant forward, his head cocked to one side, rubbing his big smooth hands together as though he were washing them. 'Roz dearest baby, I *know*! I *know*! I was at fault. I said I could not see you, as I was seeing another – about the Lord's business, as you might say.' He took a deep breath, holding his hands out now in a cat's cradle. 'I was in deep conference with our good friend and ally, Herb Roskoe, who has a hotline to almost every cable and satellite network in the Free World . . .'

59

Judge Roz Acker looked as though she'd swallowed a plum stone. 'I do not like that man, Alan. What's more, you *know* I don't like him.'

Weekes' hands writhed and slithered, his head bowed forward again. 'But dear Roz, one does not have to like a man to do business with him. Roskoe is not nice, but he is *useful*. He has influence . . . powerful friends . . .'

'You're damned right he has! Every crook and shyster in the State . . . !'

'Now that's not quite fair, Roz!'

But she was not to be stopped. 'He's a sleazeball, Weekes. An arrogant, chauvinist exploitative jerk! I heard Reagan even wanted him as an adviser on handling the media – and he'd have got it too, if the Lomax tax-scandal hadn't hit the fan first . . . No – the man's an asshole! A crooked, bigotted asshole!'

Weekes winced visibly at such obscenity on the lips of a woman. 'I grant you, Roz, he is certainly no liberal. And I agree that some of the programmes he puts out – well, some of them are vulgar, certainly – some are *very* cruel, *very* prejudiced. But when it comes to drink-driving, I'm sure you'll agree that he is most definitely on our side. And if you *do* win the Governorship, Roz, you and I will be able to cash in an awful lot of favours!'

'I'll believe that when it happens.'

'The important thing now,' Weekes persevered, 'is to get the TV networks lined up behind us against this yuppie killer, Carlton. As it's only an Inquiry tomorrow, and not a trial, we're going to want to generate as much publicity as possible. What the military would call "a softening-up" operation. Blanket coverage.

'However, we also badly need to take on board some *respectable names* . . .' Roz Acker shifted one leg over the other. Like most women in the State of California, she had good legs, good teeth, and a strong jaw. A gifted photographer could have made her look almost alluring. But where Alan Weekes was concerned, she reminded him of a knife with hair.

'Am I to assume from that, Reverend, that my organisations are somehow *not* respectable?'

Weekes' pale hands fluttered desperately. 'No, no, Roz! How could I have expressed myself so clumsily? It's just – how should I say? – horses for courses.'

'Meaning drink-drivers have to be faced down by their peers? Comfortable, white, male, middle-class? That it, Reverend?'

'Dear Roz, it's just that at this stage – at the very beginning – I feel that we must project a low profile. Not too much razzmatazz. Nothing too controversial.'

'Yeah, I read you.' Her voice was thick with contempt. 'Whatever we do, we mustn't upset Middle America, must we? As long as they're brutal, nasty and dumb, we give 'em what they want! That it?'

'Well, we do have to consider these things. It's called politics, Roz.'

'Don't patronise me, Weekes! Just tell us what favour you've curried this time.'

'Well!' The moon-face looked up and beamed. 'We have lift-off – I *think* – with a big demo at City Hall tomorrow at ten in the morning. That, I am reliably informed, is when the Carlton–McIvor case will come up – right at the top of the list, in the hope that the press won't get on to it.' He snickered. 'Well, Carlton's people obviously haven't reckoned with a few good insiders at the D.A.'s office.'

'Now,' he went on, 'as far as the bereaved father and husband is concerned, we've got Ron Sharkey to represent him – and Sharkey *always* makes waves. So there's bound to be a lot of interest – as well as interested parties.' He winked knowingly at Roz Acker. 'Certainly enough to pack the court, inside as well as out. The L.A.P.D. have been informed, of course, and I've assured them that everything will be within the law.'

They both nodded, as though this were a tiresome necessity.

'Carlton, I understand,' he went on, 'is to be represented by a smart young whizz-kid from McKenzie Brackman. Name of Kuzak – Michael Kuzak. Know him?'

She nodded. 'Yeah. Young glamour-puss. Supposed to have integrity. *Integrity?* In an L.A. law firm? *Integrity my ass!*'

The Rev. Weekes paused, trying again to conceal his disapproval of her language. Why was it she felt so obliged to express herself in those terms? Not that he would have dared criticise her. No sir! – not for all the tea in China! For to alienate the formidable Roz Acker meant not only losing the support of her myriad organisations and pressure-groups, but risked provoking the wrath of these terrible cohorts against himself. For with Roz Acker there were no neutrals.

'Naturally, our man Sharkey will go in punching, although we don't necessarily expect a decision on the first round.'

'What about Carlton's background?' Roz asked. 'Job, associations, criminal record? We've got the one drink-driving charge three years ago. There might be others. Outside the State.'

'I think we leave that sort of thing to Mr Sharkey. He may advise us to keep some of our powder dry. Remember, Carlton's not on a drink-driving rap *this* time. We must not be seen railroading him – *victimising* him. We must portray him as he is – a spoilt rich boy out with this girl, trying to impress her with his new toy – driving too fast, not looking, then . . . *whaaam!*'

Roz Acker stood up, her padded shoulders flung back, her little eyes bright and black. 'That sonuvabitch killed a woman and her child. Don't talk to me about victimisation. *That boy ain't seen nothing yet!*'

She swung on her heel.

'See you tomorrow outside the court, Reverend!'

Chapter Nine

Meanwhile, across town, the civil court was packed for the showing of the video in the case of Lowens vs. America's Most Embarrassing Practical Jokes. The usually solemn atmosphere had been replaced by an air of expectancy, as though the crowd was waiting for the curtain of a theatre to be raised. Despite air conditioning, the temperature was high. Martin Lowens dabbed cautiously at his forehead with a bandana, careful not to displace his toupee.

There was a click and some numbers flashed up on the large video monitor which had been erected in one corner. Lowens' face appeared on the screen.

'*The unification of Germany has to be considered not simply urgent but utmost to the economic future of Europe. Certainly, Soviet opposition to this result would have been uniformly met with condemnation . . .*'

'How much of this do we have to listen to?' asked Judge Lang. 'Can we fast forward?'

Lowens had been thinking how effective his speech sounded on a second hearing.

'We don't need to,' replied Sifuentes. 'It comes up pretty quickly. Soon as he starts in on Gorbachev.'

'*If Gorbachev succeeds in his reform policies, the Soviet Union* . . .'

Above Lowens' earnest face on the screen, his hairpiece twitched and started to peel back with a tearing sound.

The real Lowens turned away in embarrassment.

Sifuentes leapt to his feet. 'Let it be noted that the sound effects were added by the defendant.'

The tape ran on. '*Perestroika means pluralism, and that means opportunity for openness.*' At this, the toupee suddenly flopped down, accompanied by the sound of a car door slamming.

'*The West has to assist the Soviet Union in this process* . . .' The forelock made a vain attempt to rise against the background of a crowbar wrenching wood.

'. . . *Let me elaborate* . . .'

A shrieking whistle was heard. The toupee was whisked right off Lowens' head and dangled above his bald pate like a furry halo. A sound of muffled laughter filled the courtroom.

'*The Eastern bloc is actively promoting the spirit of friendship* . . .'

Suddenly, Lowens' head on the screen was covered again, accompanied by a thudding noise. Aware that

65

something was amiss, he patted his hair but felt everything in its right place.

Everyone was making a valiant effort to remain poker-faced. Beads of sweat were appearing from underneath the real Lowens' hairpiece as his screen image continued pontificating:

'*The Soviets cannot ignore the historical significance of East Germany . . .*' Lowens' recorded voice was almost drowned by the sound of a rocket engine firing up. Another recorded voice was superimposed: '*All systems go. We have ignition.*'

The toupee soared upwards as the rocket engines roared. The other voice commented: '*We have lift-off. We have lift-off. Uh . . . oh . . . engine trouble.*'

Most of the jury were managing to maintain their composure but they *had* to look at the screen and some were overcome by their desire to laugh. The judge was fighting a losing battle not to smile.

Lowens' voice continued. '*They cannot ignore the inevitable. Look around.*' His wig lurched wildly to the sound of a sputtering engine followed by the sound of a plane descending. Shoulders were beginning to shake. Sifuentes felt an almost over-powering urge to giggle, which he only just managed to suppress. Only Lowens looked more miserable by the minute.

'*Poland, Hungary, Czechoslovakia, the Baltic States . . . Let the Soviets see the new day – see the future.*' The wig abruptly dive-bombed back on to Lowens' head with a squelching sound.

Judge Lang could control himself no longer. He let out a huge belly-laugh, like a camel on heat – a sound made all the louder by his having tried to contain it for so long. Sifuentes rose to his feet.

'Objection! Move for mistrial.'

'Aw, come on!' spluttered the judge. 'Don't be so pompous!' He made a valiant effort to pull himself together. 'OK, OK.' Another bubble of laughter burst from him, and spread like a forest fire, sweeping across the jury, then throughout the whole court. Even the cop at the door was having to wipe away the tears.

Alone, like Horatio on the bridge, Sifuentes struggled to keep a straight face. 'Your Honour, this is prejudicial.'

'No, it's not.' Judge Lang was trying to bring himself under control, and not doing a good job of it. 'It's not. Look, the fact that everyone's laughing is not the issue. It is not relevant.' And another spluttering roar escaped from him, which he partially intercepted, so that it sounded more like a sneeze than a laugh.

'I hereby instruct the jury to take no notice of my reaction. Nor are they to . . .' Another great roar escaped from him, and Sifuentes, whose own jaw muscles were aching with the effort to remain serious, rose to his feet.

'Objection! Objection!'

'I'm sorry. I didn't mean to – it just happened. The part when the rocket took off . . .' He subsided again.

'Your Honour, I take exception.'

'OK. The court is adjourned for ten minutes.

As though this were a signal, everyone in the room – except the unhappy Professor Lowens – burst into uninhibited gales of laughter, fuelled by the solemnity of the occasion. Even Sifuentes' handsome Aztec features cracked for a moment into a grin. He walked over to Lowens. The man was sitting alone, with his head in hands, quietly sobbing.

Chapter Ten

Chuck Carlton slammed down the phone and resumed his pacing. 'Godammit! I haven't seen Janice for four days. And I haven't talked to her for two. What's the matter with her?'

'Guess she's upset,' Michael Kuzak said gently.

'Sure she's upset! *I'm* upset! But that doesn't mean we can't talk to each other. I'm holed up here – fine. We get the press off our backs. But then she goes and walks out of her job at the clinic. Doesn't tell me but leaves a message with old man Simbel, saying she's staying at her folks' cabin up on Bear Lake. No phone. Convenient, huh!'

'Try and see it from her point of view.'

'Then two days later she calls Simbel and he says I'm with you. So she calls here and says she's fine, she's coming back to L.A. tonight, and she'll be at the court

69

tomorrow. And I can't call her back because she's in a phone-box, a mile from the cabin. So thanks a lot, darling, see you in court! Does that sound like the course of true love?'

'Look, Chuck, she's a sensitive, emotional girl whose job is looking after kids. She's out on a free afternoon when suddenly she's confronted with violent death. Remember, she was the one who tried to save the kid – you were too shocked. For her the shock came later. She may well have suffered some kind of minor breakdown. And having to appear in court and go through the whole horrible scene, detail by detail . . . Well, she's probably slunk away to the most isolated place she could think of.'

Carlton had lit another cigarette, still pacing. He was too large, too restless for Kuzak's spartan beach-hut on Santa Monica. Two packets of cigarettes a day had fouled the air, which was only marginally less unpleasant than the evening smog outside. But while Kuzak was resigned to the chain-smoking, what was beginning to worry him was Carlton's drinking.

Kuzak knew that if a man wants to drink, he'll drink. It would only be useless for Kuzak to try and hide the drink – Carlton would just break out and go on a bender. But all Kuzak could do was to keep him here away from the press, on this last day before the Inquiry, and monitor his drinking.

Carlton paused by the drinks table, seemed to fidget for a moment, then poured himself a stiff vodka and tonic. He stood sipping, looking out at the hot muggy haze above the Pacific. Then he turned, grinning. 'You worried maybe I'll get pissed before tomorrow? Not even make it to the stand, huh?'

'Well I sure hope you do make it, Chuck. But if it isn't tomorrow, it'll be another day. These things don't just go away, you know.'

'I know, I know.' Carlton stared miserably into his glass. 'I wonder if *she'll* turn up? I mean, supposing she's scared of getting up there on the stand and says I wasn't paying attention . . . that I was on the wrong side of the road . . . ?'

'She's not going to do that. She'll say just the way it was. That it was an accident. Neither of you can remember *exactly* what happened. Maybe the other car was going a little fast, taking the bend. There were no tyre-marks, but that doesn't have to mean anything.'

Carlton turned from the window and stood staring moodily at Kuzak. Funny how less than ten days ago he'd have looked on the young lawyer as an equal – one of the boys, footloose and fancy-free. A good, interesting job, a Porsche and a pad on the beach in one of the most select bits of real-estate in the world.

And look at him now! For in the space of those ten days, Carlton had seemed to sag, like a balloon losing air. His perennial tan had yellowed, and where the man McIvor had punched him, his face was still puffed and greenish-yellow, with the eye small and bloodshot; while his long blond hair lay dank and lifeless against his collar, which Kuzak noticed was not quite clean.

Of course, Kuzak, with the dispassionate eye of a lawyer, realised there was nothing to be lost in Carlton looking bowed, even broken. Here was a young man in the full floodtide of life, suddenly having to live with the death of two innocent people . . . So far, so good. But it would be fatal if his client somehow managed to give the impression that he was a drinker. Not a social drinker – but a seasoned drinker, a lush. They'd look at him and think: The guy's sober now, but that next drink isn't too far away. And then they'd start wondering about that afternoon up on Benedict Canyon.

Kuzak smiled, ignoring the fresh vodka in Carlton's glass. 'I'll fix us both dinner here. Best steaks, artichoke hearts, French fries, and ice-cream and peaches. Dull but fortifying. Then an early night. I want you up on that stand tomorrow looking subdued but in good shape.'

'I'm horny as hell,' Carlton muttered. 'If only Jan would show up. For Chrissake, we *need* each other!' He started pacing again, stopping to take a drink.

Kuzak said gently, 'I guess I know as much about girls as you, Chuck. That is, I don't know exactly how they tick. But when something terrible happens – like up on Benedict – it's likely to take people in different ways. Now I can't tell you for sure why she went up to Bear Lake, but I'm darned certain it wasn't *just* to get away from you.'

He paused, realising that he was saying all this as much to convince himself as his client. For over the past few days, Carlton had dropped the odd casual remark which made Kuzak suspect that all was not well in the Chuck–Janice lovenest – even before the terrible events on Benedict. But Kuzak's brief was to shield Carlton from the press and deliver him in good order

72

to the Fatal Accident Inquiry tomorrow morning. There was nothing in the Law Association's Book of Ethics which said he had to pass judgement on his client's love life. That sort of thing was best left to Arnie Becker.

He gave Carlton a friendly locker-room grin and went on: 'We guys get pretty – well, horny – when we're cooped up and away from it. I find girls aren't like that. Sure, some are. I've known a girl have eleven guys in one night. But most girls – serious girls, like your Jan – well, sometimes they just have to get away from it all – get what they call "quiet time". No hassle, no telephone, and time to withdraw and let the wounds heal. Are you with me?'

'So-so,' Carlton growled. 'Me, I'm getting claustrophobic in here.'

'We can take a stroll on the beach.'

'Oh for Chrissake, Mike! What am I? A goddam prisoner? I haven't even been *arrested* yet!'

'Okay.' Kuzak nodded and watched Carlton heave himself up and pour another drink. He was now in that dangerous state of being neither drunk nor sober.

Carlton sat down, put his fresh drink down on the sidetable, then carefully lit a cigarette. 'You know anyone we can call up? C'mon, Mike, you must know a few numbers? Call 'em up! Get 'em out here – nice couple o' chickadees – we give 'em a nice dinner and then – whoopee!' He paused, and Kuzak noticed the dry glitter in his eyes, the moist sheen on his skin.

Kuzak said, 'My client is Arthur Simbel, I can only take instructions –'

'Aw, cut the horse-shit!' Carlton yelled, and broke his cigarette into the ashtray. 'You lawyers are so full of shit! Every minute I'm sitting here in your nice little beach-hut, the meter's running!' He leered across at Kuzak. 'How much? Two C's an hour? Three C's? And is it double away from the office?' He gave a humourless chuckle. 'Baby-sitting, huh? How you like that! Top-gun L.A. lawyer, Mike Kuzak, is paid to stay home and baby-sit ace adman Charles Carlton who's not safe on the streets! That so?'

Kuzak gave him a level stare. Carlton's eyes were beginning to lose their focus. 'Look, Chuck. I'm here to do what I consider to be in your best interests. But I have no authority over you. If you really want to go walkabout in the town, that's fine by me. I can't stop you. But if you go out in the state you're in now, and drink even more, and maybe get yourself in trouble with the cops, and they throw you in jail for the night – well, Chuck, that would be pretty well the end of the line for you. You show up at that Inquiry tomorrow fresh out of a police cell and they'll crucify you.'

'But it's got nothing to do with what happens tonight! I can screw girls and get smashed and do what I like. I've got my Constitutional Rights!' Carlton was breathing heavily. *'And I wasn't drunk when the crash happened!* That's the crux of the matter, isn't it? Or am I being dumb?' He was leaning forward, sweating. 'Tell me, Mike, am I just a dumb jerk who's going into that Inquiry tomorrow morning to get what he deserves? S'that right? You tell me.'

Kuzak noted the tone of self-pity, mingled with

truculent defeatism, and disliked both. Again he wished the girl were here, if only to try and control the man's drinking.

In one respect, of course, Carlton had been right. Kuzak was being paid handsomely for his time, with generous out-of-office expenses; and although there were no ground-rules here, he did have a duty to be level with his client.

'Chuck, the law's supposed to be precise, like a surgeon's knife. It's supposed to differentiate between what is true and not true. Between guilt and innocence. But along the way, a lot of other factors come into play. The way witnesses behave on the stand. How they look, how they talk. And you're going to be the main witness at that Inquiry tomorrow morning. You turn up with a hangover, having been brought to court by the police, and I tell you, Chuck – not even Clarence Darrow could help you!'

'But I'm innocent. Haven't done anythin'.' There was a brutish silence. 'Only an Inquiry anyway. Innit?'

'Sure, Chuck. But that Inquiry can make recommendations. And that could affect the D.A.'s office. If you make a lousy impression on the stand, and there's a lot of bad publicity, the D.A.'s office just might try to bring a charge of involuntary homicide.'

'Oh God!' Carlton's strong body suddenly sagged, shaken with irregular bursts of sobbing. 'Oh God, please help! Mike, you help me! I didn't *mean* to kill them!'

'Sure, you didn't,' Kuzak said. 'And tomorrow you're going to be able to tell them so.'

He waited until he was sure Carlton was asleep, then arranged him face-down on the sofa, pulled a blanket over him, and went into the kitchenette to prepare steak and French fries for one.

He wondered how that girl Janice had put up with him for so long. Perhaps, being a children's doctor, she liked mothering him? Better her than me! he thought.

Chapter Eleven

Outside Beverly Hills Courthouse a huge crowd had gathered, blocking traffic, spilling into side-streets, causing the usually relaxed Beverly Hills police to call urgently for reinforcements.

By 10.25 a.m. these dense ranks of demonstrators and spectators began to heave and sway, those at the back growing restless, while the front strained not to get crushed against the steps. Journalists and cameramen jockeyed for position. Telescopic lenses prodded sweaty necks. Shirts clung to perspiring backs. Sound equipment cables became snarled around feet. Tempers flared as the crowd increased, swelled by groups of women waving WADD banners and chanting in a dull, rasping lament:

'Two, four, six, eight, who do we abominate?
Four, six, eight, ten, C-A-R-L-T-O-N!'

The weather was oppressively hot. L.A.'s habitual blanket of smog, sticky and yellow, hung even lower than usual. In Kuzak's Porsche, the passenger seat was tipped back as far as possible so that Carlton was almost horizontal. Despite the heat and humidity, a rug covered him. He remembered seeing men – usually suspected terrorists or child murderers – being hustled in and out of courthouses with blankets over their heads, in order to provide spurious anonymity.

Kuzak said, 'Jeezus!'

'What's happening?' Carlton asked, genuinely bewildered.

Kuzak had been forced to stop the car several yards from the steps. He said quietly, 'Just stick close to me. Keep your face hidden and don't try to be a hero!'

An official came up and said something to Kuzak, who handed him the car keys. Kuzak then went round to the passenger side, where Carlton still lay like a corpse under the blanket. He could hear a roar as Kuzak opened the door for him.

A thin blue line of police was straining to keep the way clear to the courthouse steps. Carlton stumbled out of the car, still partly covered by the blanket, Kuzak gripping him by the arm.

Carlton now experienced a moment of total panic; it was as though he had been embroiled in some grotesque game of blind man's bluff, surrounded by mad screaming women and silent Keystone Cops. Then he heard Kuzak yell in his ear, 'Just keep on – steady as she goes!'

It was stifling, airless under the blanket; his face and

back running with sweat. There were women all round. Carlton could see their feet, mostly in track suits and sneakers; and for a brief moment, as he lifted the blanket to swallow some air, he caught a glimpse of them, their features gaunt with hatred, shaking their fists at him, pounding on the car roof, while the TV cameras bore in on him like gun barrels.

Kuzak was crouched like a full-back in a football game; and for a moment Carlton stood behind him, still partially wrapped in the blanket and quaking in his Guccis. Kuzak said, 'Right – *run!*' Carlton hugged his arms against his still sore ribs – trying to prevent further damage – and with a surge of adrenalin, head well down, he charged after Kuzak up the steps and into that courthouse.

The next twenty minutes or so passed for Carlton in a series of frenzied scenes, confused and apparently without sequence, like a badly-cut film in which he had the lead role, but no script.

The corridors were full of police and officials. Then into a courtroom, which instead of one of the smaller rooms usually reserved for accident inquiries, was one of the biggest in the building – as though chosen 'by popular demand'. The TV lights were already on, and more cables were snaking across the floor and down the aisle.

The instant Kuzak and Carlton entered an excited buzz went up; cameras flashed; and there was a great surge forwards, a sea of curious gaping faces, as a couple of policemen cleared a path for them up to the front of the court.

Carlton moved as though in a daze. It was only when he sat down that he realised that he was still clutching the blanket. He looked around. A banner had been unfurled from the spectators' gallery: painted in crude red was the legend L.A. GAYS AND LESBIANS AGAINST DRUNK-DRIVERS.

The judge, a very small dark man, banged his gavel a couple of times. 'Get that banner outta here!' he bawled. He was answered by a shrill cry, *'Discrimination!'* which he ignored.

Carlton looked around him, trying to find Janice. There seemed to be no sign of her. And then he saw McIvor. The man was sitting barely six paces away. He was wearing dark glasses, his face drawn and grey with grief, knuckles white with tension. And at that same instant he turned and looked at Carlton.

Although Carlton could not read the man's expression behind the dark glasses, he felt a crawling of the skin. He tried to look away, and thought, *How did McIvor feel looking at the person who had killed the two people he loved most in the world?* Then something happened which made Carlton want to vomit. He saw McIvor grin. It was a horrible, unnatural grin, relishing the sight of Carlton's too-handsome face still marred by bruising.

But the grin seemed to say something more: *That's nothing compared to the way you'll end up looking once I've got my hands on you again.* Then McIvor suddenly leant out, still smiling at him as though they were old friends. 'Hi Chuck! Just to let you know that you'll die in even more agony than my little Tommy.'

He had not spoken very loudly, and Carlton was not sure how many people had heard him. But Kuzak was on his feet, rigid with anger.

'Your Honour, my client has just been threatened by one of the parties to this Inquiry. Mr McIvor here has just told my client . . .'

'Objection, your Honour.' McIvor's attorney, Ron Sharkey, had risen to his feet. 'Ten days ago my client, Mr Colin McIvor, lost his wife and his five-year-old son – killed in a car driven by Mr Kuzak's client over there' – he spoke with leisured menace – 'Mr Charles Carlton –!' He turned and swept his arm to where Carlton and Kuzak sat.

Kuzak was on his feet again, struggling to make himself heard above the yells and boos and catcalls. 'Objection, your Honour!'

The judge was banging his gavel, also yelling into the uproar. 'Silence! *Silence!* If this continues, I'll clear the court. Mr Sharkey, if your client has issued a threat to anyone in this court, I shall duly enter it in the record.'

A woman's voice called from the gallery: 'What price child murder in Beverly Hills?'

'Remove that person *at once*!' the judge roared. 'If there are any more disturbances, I shall clear the court and order those responsible charged with contempt.'

Sharkey and Kuzak were still on their feet, Kuzak white with rage, while Sharkey basked in the comfortable knowledge that it was his client who would reap the harvest of sympathy. There would be no such prize for the wretched Carlton. Yet Michael Kuzak was nothing if not a fighter. He wasn't going to let this smooth,

$2,000-a-suit operator, Sharkey, win before the bell had even sounded.

The judge glared down at Kuzak. 'Mr Kuzak, you wish to lodge a formal complaint against Mr McIvor here?'

'Your Honour,' said Kuzak, 'I accept that Mr McIvor is overwrought and distressed – that this Inquiry itself is going to be a protracted nightmare, in which all the details of that tragic accident are going to be replayed in public, and that Mr Sharkey's client was not fully in control of himself when he threatened my client . . .'

The judge nodded. 'That sounds pretty fair to me. You, Mr Sharkey – have you any comments? Or shall we overlook your client's alleged remark?'

'I certainly would overlook it, your Honour,' Sharkey said, 'if I knew what this remark was.'

The judged nodded grimly. 'Since I didn't hear it myself, I rule that the incident is struck from the record. But I should remind you all – and that includes any spectators here who may be expecting some fun and games – that although this is an Inquiry and not a trial, the same rules apply.' He looked at the assistant D.A., sitting at right-angles to Carlton and McIvor. 'Mr Larsen, will you proceed with the facts, please?'

Larsen was a tall, loosely-built man who looked more like an athlete than a lawyer. He began to read from the police report. 'On the afternoon of June 25, at approximately 3.15 p.m., Beverly Hills police department received a call from a Mrs Irene Lewings, of 3490 Benedict Canyon, reporting a car smash on the canyon road, close to the turning to Stone Canyon Reservoir . . .'

Carlton again had the feeling that all this had nothing to do with him. He just sat and listened, as though watching some play on TV. The only thing that seemed real, or had any importance to him, was that he couldn't see Janice. Admittedly, the court was packed, and Carlton felt terribly exposed and vulnerable every time he turned round to look. He felt safer staring at a point mid-way between the judge and the floor.

Larsen, from the D.A.'s office, droned on, 'As far as we can establish, from the position of the two cars when the impact occurred, Mr Carlton's car – a powerful German BMW' – and a low grumbling filled the court, as Carlton put his head down and tried to sink into the floor – 'was travelling at approximately forty miles an hour on *the crown of the road* . . .'

Kuzak sprang up. 'Objection, your Honour. My client will dispute the speed of his car, and will also claim that at the last minute he tried to take evasive action, which accounts for the position of his car in the centre of the road.'

'Mr Kuzak, you will have plenty of time to try and explain your client's actions that afternoon. Mr Larsen is simply going through the facts, as they were first reported by the police.' He paused. 'I therefore hope that you are not intending to challenge every statement that is made? Your objection is overruled. Mr Larsen, please continue.'

Carlton whispered at Kuzak, 'Still no sign of Janice?'

Kuzak turned slowly, scanning the crowded court. 'I

don't see her. If she's not here by noon, I may have to call for an adjournment.'

'Is that good?'

'Neither good nor bad. It just burns up time and money.'

Larsen was saying, 'We shall be calling expert evidence on the severity of the crash, and of the appalling consequences for the two victims. Let it suffice at this point that the driver of the second car, Mrs Anne McIvor, was killed instantly, and that it took the rescue service nearly an hour to free her five-year-old child, Thomas McIvor, who died seven hours later in Washington Hospital.'

A small, choking scream went up from Colin McIvor. It seemed to operate like some kind of signal – for all at once the whole court exploded in pandemonium.

The steady chant which had been heard outside now invaded the courtroom:

'*Two . . . four . . . six . . . eight . . .*

'*Who do we abominate?*

'*Four . . . six . . . eight . . . ten . . .*

'*C. A. R. L. T. O. N . . . !*'

Judge Sachs' small face was puce with rage. 'Silence! *Silence!*' he screamed, beating out the words with his gavel. 'This – is – an – *abom -in -ation!*'

Michael Kuzak was on his feet. He spoke slowly, and not too loudly, anxious only that the judge could hear what he had to say.

'I submit, your Honour, on behalf of my client – and of justice itself – that this whole inquiry has degenerated into a squalid farce. That the demonstrations, both

84

outside and inside this court, have been deliberately and cynically contrived in order to make an example of my client. I move, therefore, that the hearing be adjourned . . .'

The judge was glaring down at him, glad to have one individual on whom he could vent his wrath. 'Are you trying to tell me, Mr Kuzak, that I am not conducting this inquiry correctly?'

'I did not say that, your Honour.'

'So what are you saying?'

'I am complaining, your Honour, that certain individuals in public life in this city are deliberately mounting a publicity campaign against my client . . . !'

'*Your client, mister, is a goddam killer!*' This from a man at the back of the court, heard by all. He was answered by a steady hand-clapping: 'Two . . . four . . . six . . . eight! Who do we abominate? *Child-killers!*'

Another ugly protracted roar which this time completely drowned out the judge's voice, even the sound of his gavel. He stood up and yelled at Larsen, 'I adjourn this hearing!' And to Kuzak and Sharkey, 'I'll see you both in my room.' Then, as an afterthought, 'Better bring your client, Mr Kuzak.'

Carlton, cringeing, terrified, felt Kuzak's reassuring grip on his arm as he was propelled towards a small door at the side of the stand.

*

85

'This isn't L.A. Law, judge,' Kuzak said. 'It's lynch law! This city hasn't seen this kind of show since the McCarthy Hearings.'

Judge Sachs glowered at them both. 'What do you have to say to that, Mr Sharkey?'

'Your Honour, this is the kind of case that's increasingly attracting moral outrage. People in this city . . .'

'My client is not – repeat *not* – on trial!' Kuzak yelled. 'We haven't even heard the evidence yet! What's the matter with you, Sharkey? You like this kind of justice, why not go practise in Albania or China!'

'I resent that,' Sharkey said slowly, his suntan turning a shade darker.

'Yeah, well, no need to get personal,' the judge said. 'Certainly this organised mayhem cannot be tolerated.' He looked at Kuzak. 'I think Mr Sharkey here does have a point.'

'Meaning?' said Kuzak.

'Well, just that these drink-drive cases . . .'

Kuzak exploded. 'You're right out of line, judge! You know damn well, and Mr Sharkey knows damn well, that Mr Carlton was tested for alcohol by Beverly Hills police *and was found to be below the limit*! Christ, the man's been pilloried in the press and on TV for the last ten days, and now he has to run the gauntlet through a crowd of half-crazed feminists, *and* he has his life threatened by Sharkey's boy . . . This is *primitive*, judge! Even by L.A. standards.'

'Okay, okay,' Sachs said, temporarily humbled, as he looked towards Sharkey for comfort. 'Things get said in the heat of the moment . . .'

'My client's whole reputation is at stake,' said Kuzak. 'Even his *life* may be at stake. And you're talking the heat of the moment – like it was some kinda domestic spat. Mr Carlton here is being railroaded – he's being murdered – he's getting the kinda justice that would give the Klan a bad name!' He turned to Carlton. 'C'mon, we'll get out the back way. Most of the mob's still in there. They can smell blood.'

'I shall reconvene tomorrow morning,' Judge Sachs said, looking very unhappy.

Chapter Twelve

'Take it easy, Mike. For God's sake! – anyone'd think you were the one getting lynched.' Brackman looked across the table at Carlton, immediately regretting the metaphor. 'Sorry, Mr Carlton.' He shook his head. 'As I was saying, we can call for a new judge, but that still leaves Sharkey and McIvor with the initiative. It just protracts matters. It also gives Chuck's enemies more time to smear him.'

'They've done that already,' Kuzak said bitterly.

Douglas Brackman sat at the head of the conference table, conveying all the *gravitas* of the firm's senior executive partner. He turned again to Chuck Carlton. Until now Brackman had only met Carlton for a few brief minutes, the day after the crash, since his old friend Arthur Simbel had called in McKenzie Brackman to handle the case.

Frankly, Brackman had not much liked what he saw. He'd found Carlton a typically arrogant, selfish young man who was too ready to see his own problems at the expense of others'. His first instinct, Brackman remembered, had been to sue the wretched Colin McIvor for the assault in the Emergency at Washington Hospital. Simbel's priority was to protect the name of his advertising agency. Neither seemed to care that two people had been killed.

Today, however, Brackman found himself looking at a completely different man. Carlton seemed to have shrunk; his face sagged, his jaw was slack, his undamaged eye bloodshot; and he had cut himself shaving. Brackman also noticed that, when he had first sat down, Carlton's hands were trembling so badly that he had to keep them under the conference table.

'Mr Carlton, there are certain facts here which have to be faced. Thanks to the First Amendment of the Constitution, and our cherished freedom of the press, we are effectively having to endure not only trial by television, but trial by the mob. I watched the TV news at midday, and I found it frankly sickening.' He looked at Kuzak. 'The question is, how do we play it from here?'

'Can we file suit against the networks?' asked Kuzak. 'Claim conspiracy to pervert the course of justice?'

Brackman steepled his fingers together, as though he were praying. 'We'd have to prove it – and although I admit we've got a pretty good *prima facie* case, getting hard evidence may not be so easy. These people aren't stupid, you know.'

'People?' said Carlton. 'What people?' He reached for a cigarette.

Douglas looked at him, almost pityingly. 'The Reverend Weekes, for a start. From what I've heard, this morning's little *grand guignol* had his fingerprints all over it.'

'You mean, the Hot Gospeller?' said Carlton. 'I caught him a couple of times on TV. Sanctimonious dick-head.'

There was a knock on the door. Roxanne Melman entered with a tray. She frowned at Carlton's cigarette smoke and set a cup before him with a disapproving air.

'Are you sure you didn't want decaffeinated coffee, sir?'

'Quite sure. I need all the caffeine I can get.'

'Won't do you any good in the long run, if you don't mind my saying so. Nicotine, caffeine . . . you'll end up with a heart attack like Mr Markowitz.'

Kuzak looked up at her.

'Thank you, Roxanne, I'm sure Mr Carlton appreciates your concern.'

Chuck took another drag on his cigarette as Roxanne left the room.

'Tell me more about Weekes. Who is he? What's his game?'

'He is not nice,' replied Brackman. 'Trouble is, he'll jump on any fashionable bandwagon that's rolling. Spiritual fervour to uplift the hearts of the oppressed minorities. Last year it was the campaign against passive smoking. Now it's drink-driving – the flavour of the month from Sacramento down to the Mexican border.'

'Do we have anything on him?' Kuzak asked.

'How d'you mean?' Brackman said.

'Dirt,' said Kuzak. 'Something to throw back at him. Weren't there some rumours some years back – about how he'd come out here from somewhere in the Mid-West – and how he'd had to leave town pretty damned quick. Talk of financial scandal – Satanic rituals – children . . .'

'Careful,' said Brackman. 'There's never been any proof. Just gossip. And I don't want McKenzie Brackman hit with a multi-million-dollar corporate libel suit. Weekes has influence in this city. He's not known as "The Cardinal" for nothing. So far, he hasn't made a personal appearance. He's hiding behind Judge Roz Acker and her hordes.'

'The lady running for State Governor?' said Carlton.

'One and the same. And a credit neither to politics, the legal profession, nor the fairer sex, in my considered opinion.'

'But I thought she was running on a feminist/Moral Majority mixed ticket,' Carlton said. 'All rapists to the electric-chair?'

'Yeah,' said Kuzak. 'And she also wants a mandatory five years' jail sentence for all drink-driving cases. And ten years, without the option, if there's a death involved.'

Carlton was lighting another cigarette, trying to control his trembling hands. He had gone very pale. He took a deep breath, exhaling slowly, and gaped at

Kuzak. 'But I wasn't drunk,' he said helplessly. 'I took the test and I was *below* the limit.'

'I know that,' Brackman said. 'We all know that. But you'd had a drink at lunch – and they can prove that. You told the cop at the scene of the accident.' He paused. 'You see, Mr Carlton, the people we're up against aren't the police, or even the D.A.'s office. Generally speaking, they play by the rules. They might – just might – try and get you indicted before a Grand Jury for reckless or dangerous driving. Though on the evidence available, with no independent witnesses, I reckon your chances would be a good deal better than even.' He glanced at Kuzak. 'What do you think, Mike?'

'I'd put it rather less than even, especially if Janice Rhodes doesn't turn up. In some ways it was lucky that the hearing broke up in confusion this morning – otherwise, I'd have had to ask for an adjournment. But if they go for reckless driving we're going to have trouble. The publicity, for a start –'

'Couldn't that backlash on Weekes and his mob?'

'Well' – Kuzak looked grim – 'We've got a dead mother and a dead child. That's one helluva scenario, Douglas. All it needs is a dead dog, and we might as well fold the hand.' He stopped. 'Sorry – that wasn't very tactful.'

Carlton was sweating, although the air-conditioning was on full, and his mouth was dry, with a rancid taste. He longed for a cold beer. A couple of cold beers. He looked at each of them in turn. 'Can they do this? I mean, can they go on night after night on TV, stuff in the papers, treating me as though I was a murderer? *Worse* than a murderer. I mean, this morning some woman in the court called me a *child murderer*!'

There was a catch in his voice, as though he were about to burst into tears. He looked beseechingly at them both. 'Look, you guys, I don't mind facing up to something I've done. And I'll take whatever they give me. A fine – even prison, maybe. But this . . . *this* . . . It's a fucking nightmare! How can you let them do this to me?'

The two lawyers were silent for a moment. Kuzak looked angry. Douglas Brackman chose his next words with care.

'We are doing all we can to ensure that you have a fair trial. You couldn't have a better attorney than Mike Kuzak. But we need your co-operation. And that co-operation includes behaving in a way that befits the circumstances. No more tantrums. And no more drinking.'

Chapter Thirteen

The restaurant was lined with dark varnished wine-barrels, imitating a cellar. Its furnishings were in that sumptuous French Empire style which some Californians mistake for good taste. The tables were large and well-spaced, each with a pair of deep red velvet wing-chairs, solid silver candelabras, silver cutlery and heavy crystal goblets. An obsequious *maitre d'* hovered around their table.

'Everything all right, *m'sieur*?'

'Yeah, terrific,' grunted Chuck. 'The whole of Southern California is baying for my blood and my girl has stood me up, but otherwise everything's fine.' After calling Janice's apartment numerous times, she had at last answered the telephone and agreed to meet him for dinner – but had she changed her mind?

At last he spotted Janice's elegant figure approaching

through the gloom of the atmospheric lighting. But as she reached his table, he was somewhat dismayed by her appearance. As usual, she was beautifully, soberly dressed, and she did not look exactly ill – but her face had a curious translucent pallor, totally bloodless, even the lips, while her eyes looked still and empty. She was gazing at a point above Carlton's head, as the *maitre d'* hauled out the heavy chair for her.

'I'm sorry. I'm late. The traffic on Sunset . . . you know . . .' Her voice trailed off, as though she had been speaking from a script and had forgotten her lines.

The *maitre d'* was fussing round her, showing her the huge menu and wine-list. Carlton smiled eagerly. 'I waited before ordering anything. The wine here is great – look, they've actually got a Chateau d'Yquem. We can have that with some raspberries for dessert.' He looked up at the waiter. 'We'll start with a bottle of Newton's Chardonnay.'

'I won't have anything to drink, thank you,' Janice said flatly. 'Just mineral water.'

The *maitre d'* hovered uneasily. '*M'sieur* would perhaps like a cocktail?'

Carlton, still smarting from Brackman's little lecture, looked anxiously at Janice. She had never approved of his drinking; on the other hand, with a few exceptions, she had never actively disapproved either. 'I'll have a Pernod,' he said smoothly, leant out and squeezed Janice's hand. It was ice-cold.

'Where've you been? I was as worried as hell when you didn't show up at the courthouse this morning.' He waited, watching her face for some trace of explanation, even sympathy. But her expression, especially her eyes, was mute and inscrutable.

'I needed some space,' she said. 'We've been spending too much time together.'

'No we haven't. You'd just been away for a week in San Francisco, remember?'

'Yes, I do remember. That's what made me realise I needed to spend some more time away from you. We need to rethink the parameters of our relationship, Chuck.'

He stared at her. 'What kind of psycho-babble is that?'

'We're going nowhere, Chuck. I realised that while I was in San Francisco. You've changed since I've known you. Before, you were fun. Now it's all money and status. And sex. The final straw was that BMW. It made you look so flashy. I'm glad it's wrecked.'

'Gee, thanks. I suppose you're glad two people died.'

Janice's face went even paler than before and her eyes filled with tears. 'That's a foul thing to say. What I meant was . . . oh, forget it.'

The food arrived, tiny portions elaborately arranged on huge plates. Again the *maitre d'* hovered by Chuck's elbow. 'Is everything all right, sir?'

'Same as it was last time,' Chuck snarled, draining his Pernod which killed the taste of the Chardonnay.

They continued to bicker over the food which Janice hardly touched. Chuck, however, suddenly felt extremely hungry; the expensive, elegant tit-bits before him just stimulated his appetite instead of satisfying it. Neither of them mentioned the accident again but their conversation was stilted. Privately, each of them craved sympathy, but got none.

Eventually, Chuck paid the bill – mentally calculating how much each mouthful had cost – and they found a cab.

Janice gave her address to the driver and turned to Chuck. 'Where are you going?'

'Where am I going? To your apartment.'

'Well . . . OK.'

'Listen, Janice, don't be like this. We've both had a hard time. Let's stand by each other. I thought I'd have a coronary when you didn't arrive at the courthouse this morning. Please don't let me down.'

He looked at her pleadingly and Janice remembered why she had been attracted to him in the first place. Somehow, his bruises made him all the more attractive – normally, he was almost too good looking.

*

It felt good to lie between the cool sheets. Outside, police sirens howled like hyenas and a helicopter with a searchlight clattered menacingly overhead in search of some unfortunate crook.

'I never felt sorry for a man on the run before,' Chuck said. 'But now I know exactly how he must feel. You can't imagine how terrible it was, all those people yelling for vengeance. You should have been there.'

'I guess it was selfish of me to go up to Bear Lake.

But I meant what I said about needing some space. You know, I did get back in time this morning but I just couldn't face going to the courthouse today.'

'But you will come tomorrow? You *must*!'

'Sure, I'll be there. But I don't know what I'll say.'

'Just tell them what happened.'

'You know, Chuck, I don't think I can remember what *did* happen. I've gone over it so many times in my mind and each time it's like a different take in a movie. Just the end is always the same. That poor kid . . . all my medical training couldn't save him. What's the point of continuing as a paediatrician?'

Tears ran down her face and into the pillow, taking traces of mascara with them. Chuck put his arm around her and stroked her back, waiting for the usual response. Nothing happened. He felt the smooth skin inside her thighs, his hand slowly moving upwards.

*

Eventually, they gave up. Janice, her earlier coolness gone, was quite affectionate but complained that her bruised ribs were made sore by Chuck's weight. Chuck, distressed that he couldn't work up his usual head of steam, was relieved though disappointed.

Janice fell asleep almost immediately. Chuck couldn't get comfortable and wandered around the apartment. He thought of returning to Kuzak's place but realised that would be an admission of failure. His macho pride, dented as it was, still persisted.

He was extremely hungry but the refrigerator contained nothing except tofu and alfalfa, plus half a loaf of San Francisco sourdough bread which was going stale. He ate it anyway, spread with tofu. It was disgusting and made him thirsty. No beer in Janice's apartment but eventually, after prowling for half an hour, he found the remains of a bottle of cooking brandy which made him even thirstier.

'What the hell did Janice mean, rethinking the parameters of our relationship?' he reflected. 'She must be going nuts. Or maybe she has someone else. Going off to Bear Lake on her own like that. *We* went to Bear Lake. Maybe she didn't go alone . . .'

Chuck dropped his aching head into his hands, then wandered to the bathroom and took a cold shower. Afterwards, he watched Janice sleeping. It reminded him of an Andy Warhol movie he'd once seen. Getting bored – as he had in the movie – he wrote on her mirror in lipstick:

SEE YOU IN COURT

Then, as dawn was breaking, he dressed and slipped out of the apartment.

To his surprise, there was quite a lot of traffic. He'd never thought of people going to work this early. In fact, he had somehow imagined that nothing happened at all until he woke – that the whole of Los Angeles ground to a halt till he, Chuck Carlton, gave the signal for the show to begin like a film director starting a crowd scene.

The cars shot past, leaving trails of exhaust fumes. Not a taxi in sight, though; and the smog was building up. Chuck's eyes, already red from too little sleep and too much cheap brandy, were smarting. He'd have to wear shades in court. Court! The thought of facing that chorus of harpies again made him sweat. Then he remembered McIvor's savage, stricken face, and remembered the real reason they were all there.

'Hey! It may never happen!' Chuck's hand was grasped by a weird guy, some kind of retired hippy. He had an impression of flowing waist-length hair, a tie-dyed T-shirt and ripped jeans. Instinctively Carlton reached for his wallet. Then a chilling fear struck him. Was this a killer hired by McIvor?

'Let me congratulate you,' said the hippy. 'I walk along here every day but I've never met another pedestrian before. An endangered species in L.A.'

Bemused, still very nervous, Chuck pulled out his wallet.

'No, I don't want money. I just wanted to say "hi". Be friendly. Not enough friends in this town. Not enough smiles. Everyone looks miserable. I smile and people think I'm crazy. Maybe I am. Must be, to stay here. You try smiling instead of looking so miserable. Like I said, it may never happen.'

'It has happened already,' Chuck said.

'In that case, you've got nothing to fear.' The hippy

raised his hand in a kind of salute and walked away. That strange image stayed in Chuck's mind and kept him going through the rest of the day.

Chapter Fourteen

Kuzak was going through the Herbstman file, combing the papers for any small details that might have been overlooked, when his intercom buzzed.

'Sure, send him in. I wondered when he'd show.'

Carlton appeared in the doorway.

'Glad to see you, Chuck. How was Janice?'

'Strange.'

'Oh?' Kuzak frowned. More than anything, he dreaded having a hostile witness on his hands. 'But she'll do her stuff today?'

'I dunno. I guess so. Said she couldn't remember exactly what happened. Said some other weird things, too.'

'Such as?' Kuzak asked.

'Oh, about how we'd have to re-examine the parameters of our relationship.'

Kuzak smiled. 'Sounds like something she picked up on that course you mentioned. The one she came back from that day . . .'

'You're right! Why didn't I think of it before.' Carlton beamed with sudden enthusiasm. 'Well, let's hope for the best!'

Kuzak nodded, wondering at his client's naive optimism. 'I hope she won't become a hostile witness. We need her help, Chuck.'

Putting aside the Herbstman file, Kuzak went over the details of Carlton's case and rehearsed some answers to the questions which Ron Sharkey, McIvor's attorney, might ask.

Then they set off for the court. As they got into the elevator, they collided with a delivery man carrying a large cardboard box marked *Dairyland*.

*

This time, Chuck sat as upright as the Porsche passenger seat would allow. No hiding under a blanket today. Although his night with Janice had been a sexual disaster, he had at least made contact with her, and knew that with a little patience he could win her back completely. He had also been strangely comforted by his encounter at dawn with the hippy philosopher.

Once again, they ran the gauntlet of the WADD and GLADD demonstrators, carrying the same banners and chanting their mechanical dirges, like a Greek chorus. But somehow they seemed less threatening the second time round. Carlton glimpsed a group at the top of the steps, carefully standing in line with a TV camera crew. They were dressed in boiler-suits, with hair like badly mown lawns, and were carrying a banner:

ALL MEN ARE RAPISTS
ALL MEN ARE DRUNK DRIVERS
ALL MEN ARE KILLERS

As he came level with them, Carlton raised two finger and – fatally – laughed. Kuzak was close to him, but looking in the other direction, trying to catch a glimpse of the Reverend Weekes. But the mob's spiritual leader was again lying low, so Kuzak had also missed Carlton's performance before the TV cameras.

Inside the courtroom things seemed to be less hectic, less threatening than yesterday, and Chuck was relieved to see Janice already seated. She looked cool and elegant despite the heat, in a large hat and sunglasses. Her pale face was immobile but her nose was pink and she frequently dabbed under her glasses with a paper handkerchief.

Judge Sachs bustled into the courtroom and banged his gavel on the table. 'Today we are going to conduct this hearing in an orderly fashion. Anyone steps outta line and I'll clear the court. Is that absolutely understood?'

Carlton noticed there was no sign of McIvor or his attorney, Ron Sharkey.

*

As Janice took the stand, there was a low murmur across the court. Judge Sachs scowled down at the serried ranks below him. 'I will *not tolerate* any attempt to either interrupt or intimidate this witness! Your witness, Mister Kuzak.'

Kuzak treated her with great care. He knew that the outcome of the inquiry depended on her.

'You are Dr Janice Rhodes, and you live at fourteen-two-0, Oakland Drive, Pasadena?'

'Yes.'

'And you are a qualified paediatrician at the San Fernando Clinic for Children?'

'Yes.'

'How old are you, Dr Rhodes?'

'Twenty-nine.'

'And how long have you known Mr Charles Carlton?'

'Nearly five years.'

'So we can assume that you know him as well – even better, perhaps – than anyone alive?'

There was a sudden deep hush. Kuzak waited, looking straight at her as though trying to hypnotise her back into speech. Instead, she just gazed at something high up and far away. 'Dr Rhodes, I asked you . . .'

Slowly she looked down at him, her face utterly

expressionless. In a small, still voice she said, 'Yes?'

Kuzak concealed his irritation. 'I suggested to you, Doctor Rhodes, that you know Mister Charles Carlton here extremely well?'

'Yes, I know him quite well.'

Kuzak's irritation was being replaced by panic and dismay. 'Dr Rhodes, you were with Mr Carlton on the afternoon of Thursday, the 25th?'

'Yes.'

'What were you doing that afternoon?'

'We were driving back . . .' She paused, and there was another murmur across the court, as heads turned, necks craned towards the doors at the back. Supported on each arm by a court official, and led by the bulky figure of Ron Sharkey, was Colin McIvor. He was ashen-faced, wearing dark glasses again, and seemed on the verge of total collapse.

Kuzak watched their entrance with growing fury. Until now he had been inclined to believe that McIvor deserved a good deal more sympathy than his own client, Carlton, who was threatened with probably nothing more than a suspended driver's licence and a few days' nasty publicity.

He now began to revise this view. For what they were now seeing was a well-rehearsed ploy to win sympathy from the court, and at the same time to eclipse Janice's testimony from the stand.

Kuzak also knew there was nothing he could do to counter such a ploy – indeed, any attempt to do so, and thus question McIvor's motives, would only increase sympathy for the man, as well as putting both Kuzak and Carlton in an even dimmer light than before.

There was nothing for it, Kuzak decided – just bite on the bullet and keep going.

'Dr Rhodes, you were telling us about the afternoon in question – how you were driving with Mr Carlton in his car?' He paused, but there was no reaction from her. 'You were driving with Mr Carlton along Benedict Canyon? Is that correct?'

She just nodded. Judge Sachs leaned over and said, in his most soothing voice, 'I appreciate how upsetting this must be for you, Dr Rhodes – but if you *could* just try and speak up a little . . .'

Kuzak nodded his appreciation to Judge Sachs, for this was the best moment in the hearing so far – at least, from his client's point of view. He turned to Janice and smiled.

'In your own words, Dr Rhodes, can you tell us what happened that afternoon?'

Janice seemed poised to answer when a deep, horrible choking noise came from the front row, barely a dozen paces from where Kuzak was standing. It was Colin McIvor, slumped in his chair next to Ron Sharkey, his face streaked with tears from under his dark glasses, his body heaving with apparently uncontrollable grief.

Kuzak thought: In a city that lives by ham-acting, this was surely an Oscar performance! But for the moment he had to go on coaxing this beautiful girl into giving some sort of account of that terrible afternoon.

'Can you remember at all what happened, Dr Rhodes? How it was just *before* the crash?'

'I don't really remember it at all.'

'Can you say, maybe, what speed you were doing?'

'No. That is, I don't know. I'm no good at judging speeds.'

If she keeps this up, thought Kuzak, she might as well wrap the poor bastard up and send him to the D.A.'s office direct.

But he managed to smile encouragingly. 'I don't want you to tell us *exactly*, Dr Rhodes . . .'

Sharkey stood up. 'Objection. Counsel is attempting to distract the witness from giving an accurate answer.'

'Mr Sharkey, not everyone in the State of California is as fluent with the language as yourself. At least allow Dr Rhodes a little latitude in answering the questions. Objection overruled.'

Kuzak nodded his appreciation, then turned again to Janice. 'Could you say, very *roughly*, what speed the car was doing?'

'I'd say –' She stood staring into the middle distance. 'I'd say, maybe –'

Kuzak's heart was pounding. 'Yes?'

'Well, it was a fairly quiet road, so I'd say we were going fairly fast.'

Kuzak ground his teeth. *For God's sake, woman, what are you trying to do? Get him a stretch of three-to-five for driving recklessly, with the likelihood of endangering life?*

There was a satisfied murmur throughout the court. The punch had landed and even Carlton knew that he was hurt – badly hurt – and not by the police or the

D.A.'s office, but by his own lovely Janice who never believed in hurting anyone.

For a moment he sat gaping at her, unbelieving, while Kuzak pressed on at his thankless task.

'What speed would you call *fairly fast*, Dr Rhodes?'

She stood very pale, and seemed to be searching for the answer somewhere high up near the roof of the court. When she finally answered, her voice was clear and flat, without a trace of emotion.

'I'd say fifty was quite fast.'

'But how fast do you think you were going that afternoon?'

'I'd say maybe a bit less than fifty. There wasn't much traffic, you see.'

'Would you say you were doing less than forty . . . ?'

'Objection, your Honour,' said Sharkey. 'Trying to lead the witness . . .'

'Yeah, you gotta let your witness answer in her own words, Mr Kuzak. Objection sustained.'

Kuzak turned again to Janice. 'Can you remember what happened when the other car appeared?'

'The other car?'

'Yes, the one you crashed into?' And suddenly it occurred to Kuzak that the girl was on some drug, some heavy tranquilizer – she was a doctor, after all, so it would be no problem. No problem for *her*, that is, he thought – but a very big problem for my client. Kuzak watched, waiting.

'I'm sorry,' she said finally, 'I just don't remember anything very much before we got to the hospital. I think I was suffering from shock.'

Kuzak turned to the judge. 'I have no further questions, your Honour.'

Judge Sachs nodded. 'Mr Sharkey – your witness.'

'Thank you, your Honour.' Sharkey smiled at Janice, a smile that said, You're a honey and you're my witness, so let it flow . . .

'Dr Rhodes, on the day in question, had you and Mr Carlton had a long, good lunch . . . ?'

'Objection!'

'Sustained. Mr Sharkey, although this is only an inquiry, you must know you cannot lead the witness . . .'

'I withdraw the question, your Honour.' Sharkey looked again, gloatingly, at Janice. 'Now, Doctor, could you tell us what you and Mr Carlton did during the three or four hours before the accident?'

'Yes. We had lunch with the head of Chuck's advertising agency.'

'Where did you have lunch?'

'The Beau Sejour on Wilshire.'

Sharkey nodded appreciatively. 'Nice, very nice! And what did you drink, Dr Rhodes?'

'Me?' She looked startled.

'You – and Mr Carlton.'

Kuzak jumped up. 'Objection, your Honour! Evidence will be produced that my client submitted to an alcohol-breath test as soon as the police arrived on the scene, and that the result was negative. Mr Carlton was *below the legal limit*.'

'Sustained. Mr Sharkey, you don't need me to tell you what's admissible and what is not in this type of inquiry.'

'I thank your Honour.' Sharkey gave a slightly exaggerated bow to the judge, then turned again to Janice.

'I was under the impression that Mr Carlton had in fact drunk alcohol shortly before the accident. Can you now confirm that he had in fact drunk nothing that day?'

Kuzak was up again. 'Objection!' – then rounded in a fury on Sharkey – 'You know damn well how much my client had drunk! It was all in the police report.'

'I am indebted to you, Mr Kuzak,' Sharkey said smoothly. 'I was under the misapprehension that your client had in fact *drunk nothing*. However, I stand corrected.'

Kuzak found himself rapidly losing control, both of himself and of his client's case. For he knew from experience that while a judicious display of anger could often win over the court, to lose one's temper completely was usually fatal. He counted up to ten, slowly, under his breath, then faced Judge Sachs.

'Your Honour, I submit that Mr Sharkey's line of questioning is not only unfair and unethical, but is also against the spirit of natural justice . . .'

'Objection!' boomed Sharkey.

'Sustained! Mr Kuzak . . .'

But Kuzak felt a wind in his sails, and he was not going to back down now. Judge Sachs was banging his gavel, and a loud murmuring sound swelled up in the courtroom. Kuzak had to shout to make himself heard.

'Mr Sharkey has introduced into this inquiry a malicious and deliberately misleading fact – that my client had had *one glass of wine* with lunch that day . . .'

'Are you contesting that evidence, Mr Kuzak?'

'I am not contesting it as a fact . . .'

Judge Sachs frowned. 'Then what is your point, Mr Kuzak?'

'. . . Mr Sharkey is trying to smear my client by *suggesting he was drunk . . .* !'

'*Objection!*' Sharkey yelled: 'I demand an apology from Counsel!'

Judge Sachs glared down at both attorneys. 'Mr Kuzak, you do your client no favours by insulting other members of this court.'

'Very well. I thank your Honour.' Kuzak half turned to the court. 'I would also ask that the Prosecution refrain from introducing extraneous and irrelevant facts.'

'Yeah, okay – sustained. Mr Sharkey, I think we should stick to the facts of the case. Continue . . .'

Big deal! thought Kuzak. If I hadn't objected, he'd have allowed Carlton's driving ban three years ago to have gone into the record.

'Dr Rhodes, with your experience of Mr Carlton, would you describe him as a stable, home-loving man?'

'Objection!' Kuzak's temper was beginning to fray, growing weary of the legal jargon. 'Your Honour, all this has nothing whatsoever to do with the case. It is devious, irrelevant, and intended simply to mislead the Inquiry.'

'Sustained.' Sachs glared down at them both again. 'Will Counsel approach the Bench, please. Mr Sharkey – Mr Kuzak' – his voice had dropped to an angry whisper – 'I don't know exactly what's going on here –'

Kuzak could control himself no longer. '*You* may not know, your Honour, but just about any reasonably intelligent person would know – and would know that these proceedings are a travesty . . .'

'What did you say, Mr Kuzak?' Sachs gaped at him, scarcely believing his ears.

'I said that this court is a travesty of justice . . .'

'Resume your place!' Sachs squealed, puce with rage.

'. . . Would know,' Kuzak went on, 'that my client here is being fitted up . . .'

'*What did you say, Mr Kuzak?*'

'I said that my client is being fitted up as an irresponsible drunkard . . .'

'Mr Kuzak – if you do not this instant resume your place, I will cite you for contempt of court!'

'You couldn't. This court is *beneath* contempt!' He turned to Carlton. 'Let's go!'

Then to Janice, still on the stand. 'It's been nice meeting you, Doctor!'

With that, Kuzak put his head down and charged like a bull, his hands ready to contend with anyone who tried to stop him. Carlton rose to his feet, confused, glancing at the enraged Judge Sachs, then at Janice, who studiously avoided his eyes.

Sachs was beating his gavel again, yelling for silence. Carlton saw the whole court watching him.

Kuzak had reached the doors, his fists clenched, knowing that if he didn't get out now, he might lash out at somebody, anybody, and so ruin his own career, as well as his client's.

Carlton stood for a moment transfixed. He was waiting for someone to give him a signal – the judge, Janice perhaps . . . Behind him came a surging roar of mock applause, whistles and catcalls, punctuated by Judge Sachs' frenzied banging of his gavel.

Then Carlton panicked. With his head down, and keeping his eyes on the floor, he charged after Kuzak. Women's voices sounded in his ears. 'Chicken . . . !'

'He's running for it . . . !' 'Yuppie killer . . . !' – And there was taunting laughter.

Carlton reached the court doors, just in time to hear Judge Sachs' yelling voice declare that the hearing was adjourned.

Chapter Fifteen

The two of them emerged on to the steps of the court-house. They were instantly pounced on by several gangs of newsmen and TV crews, while below, behind a temporary police barrier, was the same hostile milling crowd. In the hazy smog they appeared to Carlton to stretch to infinity.

'. . . d'ya feel, Mr Carlton . . . your attorney walking out like that . . . ?'

'Mr Kuzak, you got thrown into jail last year, on a point of principle . . . Right?'

'Mr Carlton, any idea why your friend, Dr Rhodes, gave evidence as she did?'

Carlton saw that the last interviewer was a very pretty dark girl, standing with a microphone in front of one of the TV crews. He said aggressively, 'She was in shock. She said so, didn't she?'

The girl arched her eyebrows, and gave a sceptical smile. 'Would you describe her evidence as helpful, Mr Carlton?'

Kuzak was next to him, holding his arm. 'Don't say anything! Leave this to me.'

Kuzak then positioned himself strategically in line with as many cameras and microphones as he could summon. 'I'd like to say first that in nearly a decade of working as an attorney in this city, I have never – *repeat never* – experienced such naked perversion of justice . . .'

But the cameras were not so interested in Kuzak; they wanted Carlton. 'Can you comment on that, Mr Carlton? Did you feel it was *naked injustice*?' The journalists were already sniffing a headline phrase.

'Ask my attorney. I'm not taking questions.'

'Mr Carlton, you seemed in a pretty good mood when you went into court this morning . . .'

Carlton stared at him, narrowing his eyes against the acid glare of the smog. He recognised one of L.A.'s best-known TV reporters. 'In a good mood?' he repeated. 'Yeah,' the TV man said, smiling. 'You went in all jaunty, laughing and making rude gestures to the good ladies of the W.A.D.D.' – he turned to the camera – ' "Women Against Drunk-Driving." ' Then back to Carlton. 'Don't you remember?'

'No, I don't remember, and I have nothing to say.'

Kuzak grabbed his arm. 'C'mon, let's get outta here!'

The pretty woman reporter pushed forward. 'Next time will you be treating Dr Rhodes as a hostile witness, Mr Kuzak?'

116

Kuzak paused, his mind inflamed by the events of the afternoon. 'Get this straight. I was appearing today on behalf of a witness in a Fatal Accident Inquiry. My client, Mr Carlton, is totally innocent. He was tested for alcohol, and found to be below the limit. Since then no charges have been made against him. I am confident that no charges will be brought. And yet today my client has been treated as a common criminal – as though he'd already been found guilty . . .'

At that moment there was an excited babble round the doors of the court. It was a grand entrance of a movie queen. Janice walked straight ahead, her wide-brimmed hat shading her face, her eyes still remote and expressionless. The reporters and cameramen swarmed round her, finally succeeding in blocking her progress.

'. . . Did you really remember nothing? . . . Will you be happy, Doctor, to go through all this again? . . . How d'ya feel about Mr Carlton? . . . You and Mr Carlton gonna get married?'

This last question, futile though it was, seemed completely to undermine Janice. She let out a cry of misery, brought out her handkerchief, clasped it across her mouth and started to struggle through the ranks of reporters.

Carlton suddenly felt a great wave of affection come over him, an urge to protect her, to guard her from these media jackals.

He reached her, no longer caring whether the cameras were on them both or not. He touched her hand. 'Jan, darling . . . !'

She blinked, saw who it was, and said quietly, 'Not now. Please. I just want some *space*. I don't want to talk to you right now. I'm not feeling well . . .'

Kuzak grabbed his arm again. 'Leave it until you're both alone, Chuck. For Chrissake, this is turning into a soap-opera!' He was already hustling Carlton away, down the steps, when there was another rustle of excitement from the courthouse doors, and most of the media moved away from Carlton and Kuzak, swarming on to their fresh victim.

Carlton was just able to see, beside the bulk of Ron Sharkey, the white face of Colin McIvor.

*

'Yes, Mr Petersen, I do understand. It's very kind of you. Please may I put you on hold for a moment? . . . Good afternoon, McKenzie Brackman . . . I'm sorry, Mr Kuzak is on the other line . . . No, his secretary isn't available but I'll have him call you as soon as he's free . . . So you see, Mr Petersen, it's a question of space. We have a small refrigerator here and – oh, excuse me . . . Good afternoon, McKenzie Brackman . . . No, his line is still busy . . . – we now have five dozen quart tubs of yoghurt here, Mr Petersen, and it's starting to go bad. We can't eat it fast enough . . . Yes, we know it's an excellent product. Just one moment, please . . .'

Roxanne Melman flicked the switch to 'hold' again, put her hands up to her head and groaned.

'Having problems, Roxanne?' asked Abby as she approached the reception desk.

'You might say so. Esther is throwing up in the ladies' room so she asked me to take over the switchboard. The phones are going crazy and so am I.'

'What's the matter with Esther?'

'She ate some guacamole-flavoured yoghurt in her lunch break.'

'What!'

'This guy Petersen, the Dairyland man, won't take no for an answer. Every day he sends Ann Kelsey more and more yoghurt. They've started this new line of savoury flavours. They're disgusting! If he goes on like this she'll be prosecuting instead of defending him. Hey, he's still on hold . . . Excuse me, Mr Petersen, a long distance call has just come through so I have to go. But please – no more yoghurt. Goodbye.'

Meanwhile, Abby had opened a tub of chilli-flavour yoghurt. 'Yes, I see what you mean. *Blech*!' She held it out to Roxanne. Esther was tottering back from the ladies' room. When she saw Abby proffering the tub, she wheeled sharply and retraced her steps at a run.

'You know something, though,' Roxanne said. 'Last night I put some of the cucumber-flavour stuff on my face and it was better than a session at the beauty parlour!'

'Maybe you've made a discovery there,' said Abby. 'I'll try that tonight.' She dipped a finger into another

119

tub. 'You know, this alfalfa flavour isn't bad at all. Try some.'

Roxanne opened another tub. 'Oh *no!*' she shouted. 'It's true! There *is* something in there!'

'What!?'

'Ugh! It's . . . worse than a slug.'

'What could be worse than a slug? No, don't tell me.'

'It's a cigarette butt.'

'Yecchhhh!'

The telephone rang unheeded as Abby and Roxanne bent up double and mimed the symptoms of acute food-poisoning – a performance only marred by paroxysms of giggling. They were still doing this, when the door opened and Michael Kuzak and Chuck Carlton walked in.

'Anyone doing any work round here?' asked Kuzak. 'Because if you are, I sure wouldn't want to disturb you!'

He was still smarting with anger from the events of the afternoon.

'Sorry, Mike,' said Abby. 'We were just sampling some forensic testimony –'

As she spoke, Roxanne exploded with half-stifled laughter.

'What the hell is it?' Kuzak yelled, and looked anxiously towards Carlton. This was just about the worst impression the firm could give his client. One of their attorneys and the secretary laughing themselves half-sick, while Kuzak's own client was being subjected to a flagrant distortion of justice.

Abby met his eyes, trying not to giggle. 'The Petersen

120

case, Mike. You know, the slug in the Dairyland yoghurt tub.' She paused. 'It does have its comic side to it.'

'I'm glad someone has time to get a laugh in this place,' Kuzak said, then turned to Roxanne. 'Tell Douglas we're here. He's expecting us.'

Carlton stood patiently, swallowing hard, longing for a glass of beer. They must have *some* in the office. While Roxanne spoke on the intercom to the senior partner, Carlton turned to Kuzak. 'Is it possible to get a beer here? I'm parched. All that tension . . .'

Abby looked enquiringly at Kuzak, then at Roxanne. 'Do we? I don't know . . .'

Roxanne said, 'Iced water, coffee, decaff, soda. But alcohol, no. Or maybe you'd like a salmon-flavoured yoghurt!' And she and Abby again collapsed into helpless laughter.

'Is there something to celebrate?' Douglas Brackman stood in the doorway, his face emanating magisterial gloom.

Abby understood this was neither the time nor the place to be seen enjoying a joke. 'I'm sorry, Douglas.' She turned to Kuzak and Carlton. 'Good day, Mike – Mr Carlton.' And she swept out of the room. Brackman said, 'Right! It's time this firm got down to some serious lawyering. So let's go!'

Chapter Sixteen

The TV set was in a small room off the main body of offices, reception and interviewing chambers, which was known as the QUIET ROOM. It was never used for recreation, and only watched when – as now – something was scheduled to appear that might have some bearing on a case the firm was handling.

There were only a few upright chairs, none of them very comfortable. Kuzak and Carlton sat in the front, Brackman behind. The video-recorder started to run while the ads were still coming up. Kuzak said, by way of lowering the tension, 'We'll be getting videos of all newsflashes that relate to our case. This is just to give us a flavour of what we're in for.'

If this was meant to reassure Carlton, it failed. He got out his cigarette case and was about to light up, when Brackman touched his shoulder. 'I'm sorry, Mr

Carlton, but we have an office rule – no smoking.'

'Shit,' Carlton said, as the credits for the early news began to roll.

Brackman and Kuzak exchanged glances, while Carlton morosely returned the cigarette case to his pocket.

They watched News from the Middle East; the floor of the House of Representatives; a three-minute feature on how the Soviets were again running out of food. So far, so good.

Kuzak said, 'The further down the agenda, the better for us.'

But as he spoke, there was a long shot of the Beverly Hills courthouse – the crowd of demonstrators round the steps, a banner reading: ALL DRINK-DRIVERS ARE MURDERERS! – all to the harsh overlay of a woman's voice: '. . . *Feelings are running high in Beverly Hills today, as the first day of the Fatal Accident Inquiry ended when one of the attorneys, Michael Kuzak, stormed out of court with his client, successful advertising executive, Chuck Carlton . . .*'

All this against freeze-frame close-ups, first of Kuzak, then of Carlton – laughing on his way into court – but with no sign of the harpies with their sign: ALL DRIVERS ARE MURDERERS!

Carlton sunk his head in his hands and moaned. 'Oh God, this is awful . . . !'

The commentary continued. '. . . *leading to the deaths of 28-year-old Mrs Anne McIvor, who died instantly, and that of her five-year-old son, Tommy, who died later in hospital.*'

There was a shot of McIvor being helped out of the

123

court, leaning on Ron Sharkey, who seemed to be shielding him from the crowd. '*My client is, of course, deeply shocked . . . And may I express my absolute disgust at the conduct of Mr Carlton's attorney, Mr Michael Kuzak. Mr Kuzak, and his carefree young client, seem to think that this horrible case should, in some way, be used by Mr Kuzak to enhance his reputation as one of L.A.'s most glamourous attorneys . . .*'

'How can they?' cried Carlton. He looked beseechingly at Kuzak, then at Brackman. 'They're making out that I was trying to grandstand! It wasn't like that . . .'

On the screen the attractive young woman-reporter was interviewing the stricken McIvor: '*I realise, Colin, that all this must be terribly painful . . .*'

McIvor, behind his impenetrable dark glasses, looked like a waxwork. He stared straight into the camera and said, '*I've got nothing left. Does that bastard realise that . . . ?*' He choked on his tears. '*You'd think he might have said he was sorry, written a note or something . . . He wipes out a whole family, then he hires some schmuck to insult the judge, and then they both walk out – like they're the wronged party! I just can't believe people could be so callous!*'

Kuzak now appeared, briefly. '*Once again dashing young attorney, Michael Kuzak, has barnstormed the proceedings . . . Mr Kuzak, could you tell us . . .*'

Kuzak said, '*I've been an attorney in L.A. for nearly ten years. And today's proceedings have been a travesty of justice . . .*'

This was followed by a close-up of Janice, who was introduced as '*Glamourous Dr Rhodes, of Pasadena, who is a long-time partner of Carlton's'* – and here was the same freeze-frame of Carlton laughing, then back to the close-up of Janice on the steps. '. . . *Who was a passenger in his car when the crash occurred. Dr Rhodes, who is a paediatrician with the San Fernando Clinic –*' Carlton sucked in his breath. 'Jesus, they're not going to like that!'

'. . . *was thus able to try and save little Tommy McIvor. But sorrowfully in vain.*' The microphone was thrust into her face.

'. . . *Did you find it very difficult giving evidence today?*'

She stared blankly at the interviewer.

'*Did you feel overwhelmed by it all?*'

'Aw shit!' said Kuzak. 'Those lowlife journos – !'

On the screen they watched Janice put her hand up to her eyes, under the wide-brimmed hat, and appeared to wipe a tear away.

'. . . What are they trying to do to us?' roared Kuzak. '*Arrivederci* justice!' And he plunged his head into his hands.

Carlton was trying to follow what Janice was saying on-screen. '*I just want to try and forget it all and rebuild my life.*'

'*With Mr Carlton?*'

For a moment she looked as though she had not understood the question. '. . . *I'm sorry, I have no comment on that . . .*'

The woman-reporter now facing the camera, controlled and competent. '*After the break I'll be talking to a man who has very strong opinions about what he calls "Death Drivers" . . . The former judge and now Republican Candidate for the Governorship . . . Roz Acker . . . !'*

'Do I have to watch any more of this crap?' Carlton said wearily.

'We'll leave the video running,' Brackman said, and turned off the set. 'Just in case we catch that bitch Acker making a defamatory statement.' He looked gloomily at Kuzak. 'I begin to understand, Mike, why you blew your stack in there today.'

'Thanks!' Kuzak jerked his thumb at the TV. 'But hell, that was nothing! You should have been in court!'

'We'll get a transcript,' Brackman said, standing up. He looked at Carlton. 'Judge Sachs has designated a new hearing for a week today. In the meantime I suggest you get through to that nice girl of yours, and maybe . . .'

'Yeah?' Standing up, Carlton was at least one inch taller than Brackman, who was certainly no pygmy. 'What, *Mister* Brackman?' Carlton was very tired, and very angry, as well as a little desperate. Just then he felt like taking a swing at Brackman, who seemed to be suggesting that Janice was out of line. Strangely, Janice was the one person whom Carlton did not blame for the day's disaster. The fact that she had effectively recited to him a 'Dear John' letter on the evening's TV bulletin appeared not to have fully registered. He measured Brackman, eye-to-eye.

'Just tell me! What do I say to my girl? You wanna write the script?'

'Take it easy, Chuck,' Kuzak said.

Brackman shrugged. 'I'll be seeing you, Mike. Mr Carlton.' He nodded and slipped quickly from the room.

Carlton let his breath out in a long tight hiss. He found he was shaking all over. He wanted a cigarette and a drink. *God, he wanted a drink!* His brain and whole nervous system were screaming for one. He looked defiantly at Kuzak, then took out his cigarette case. 'You wanna stop me?' he growled.

'Take it easy, Mike.'

'Aw hell. It's okay for you. You walk outta court, get a lot of publicity – what the hell!' He lit a cigarette and took a long deep drag. 'Me, I'm left in the shit – right up to my eyeballs.'

'You've gotta try and look on the plus side,' – trying to convince himself as much as his client – 'There comes a point when the publicity starts backfiring on the other side. People don't like seeing a guy railroaded by the media and a few unscrupulous politicos and pressure-groups.'

'Like hell they don't! They love it! They want me dead! They want me grovelling, apologising to the nation – and all because I had a glass of wine for lunch *and was under the legal limit*. That's why they hate me! Because I slipped through the net – because I haven't made it easy for them. I'm innocent, for Chrissake! I wasn't even on trial back there . . .' His voice cracked with emotion and he reached for another cigarette . . .

Kuzak, conscious that the small room was now full of cigarette smoke, sighed. 'Look, Chuck, I don't

127

wanna be a killjoy, but I have to insist that you don't smoke anymore.

Carlton scowled, hesitating. 'Is it a criminal offence with you guys?'

'Pretty damn near is,' Kuzak said, grinning. 'They're all on one helluva health kick back there, so that some days I get to the office and expect to find a Quakers' meeting going on!' He was still grinning, trying to buoy up Carlton's morale – for he knew, from bitter experience, that a client whose morale cracks is, more often than not, dead in the water.

'Let's continue in my office,' Kuzak added. 'We're less likely to be disturbed.'

'You guys work pretty late, huh?'

'Sure. Some of us.'

'And the meter's on?' They had reached Kuzak's office. Carlton was leering at him, as the door was opened for him. Kuzak led the way in and sat down.

Carlton said again, 'I asked if the meter was still on? You know, clickety-click, at five bucks a minute?'

'Your boss, Arthur Simbel, hired us. If you're worried about it, you should ask him.'

'Sure. Trying to keep the agency's nose clean. Isn't that it?'

Kuzak gave him a level stare. 'It's a perfectly good motive.'

'Yeah, you spin it out, and maybe you keep the agency and maybe you don't. But all the same, isn't it? Whatever happens to me, I'm just another commodity

128

– a poor Joe that got his car smashed up and is branded thereafter as a child murderer. So much for Californian justice.'

Kuzak had a slim gold pencil in his hand and was tapping on the desk-top like a metronome. 'You may not believe me, Chuck, but that's why I do this job. I do it because I *care*. I care about my clients and care about Californian justice.'

Carlton sat down. The air-conditioner was pumping out dry stale air which was giving him a sore throat. He felt cold and clammy, and wondered if he was going down with the 'flu.

'One thing I want to get absolutely clear,' Kuzak said. 'I was as disgusted as you about what happened today.'

'*You* were disgusted! Sure. It's easy for you – you're part of the system, you make the right noises, you make a scene in court then storm out and get yourself on TV and in all the papers . . .'

'Okay, okay. You don't have to believe me. But since your boss is paying for my time, let's get down to some essentials. I want to talk to you about your friend, Janice.'

'What about her?' Carlton snapped.

'I think it would be fair to say that she didn't do you any favours today.'

'Well, what the hell! She was in shock – she said so. She tried to help the kid. She did everything she could. Believe me!'

'I'm sure she did. It's just a pity she didn't do the same for you at the hearing today.'

Carlton glared at Kuzak, then got out his cigarettes again. 'You gonna try and stop me?'

Kuzak gave a resigned shrug. 'Look, Chuck. You're in one helluva jam – and if today is anything to go by, it's not going to be easy to get you out of it.'

'That's what you're paid for, isn't it?'

'Yes, that is what I'm paid for. But I can't succeed without your help. And that means your girl, too.'

'Why d'you have to go on bringing her into it?'

Kuzak watched him light his cigarette with trembling hands, then suck in the smoke with all the single-mindedness of a junkie.

'I'm not bringing her in, Chuck. She's already in. She was our star witness. And she blew it. I want to know why?'

'Well why not ask her?'

Kuzak could feel the hostility crackling across the desk. 'I may have to,' he said grimly. 'But I'd prefer you to.'

There was a long pause. Carlton inhaled with his head back, eyes closed. 'You want to know *why* she blew it? Right?'

'Right on the button, Chuck!'

'I dunno. Honest. She's a very moody girl – very highly strung.'

'Enough to drop you in the shit, like today?'

'It wasn't her that dropped me in it – it was that goddam judge!'

'Okay, the judge didn't help. And I'm going to apply for a new one at the next hearing. But that still leaves your girl.'

Kuzak sat waiting. He didn't want to put words in his client's mouth. He wanted Carlton to tell it how it was. But Carlton said nothing, just sat with his profile upturned, his eyes closed, smoking greedily.

'Chuck, I have to ask you this. You and Janice were the only witnesses to the crash. Is there something you haven't told me? Something that only Janice and you know about, but don't want to make public?'

Carlton half opened his eyes, still leaning back. 'What are you suggesting?'

'I'm asking. I'm asking what happened to you and Janice which you don't want made public?'

Carlton sat up again with a start. 'There was nothing. Nothing at all!'

'Then why did she behave as she did today?'

'I told you – shock. She'll get over it.'

'I hope she does – for your sake.'

'Hell, you don't know her. She's a very beautiful human being.'

'I'm sure she is. She also crapped on you from a great height today. I want to know why?'

'I told you!' Carlton said. 'She was in shock and couldn't remember. Right?'

'No, Chuck. Not right at all.' He looked at Carlton through the haze of cigarette smoke. 'I can't help you if you won't *help me* to help you.'

'How were you getting on *before* the crash?'

'You live at separate places. Were you getting on well in bed?'

Carlton stood up. 'I bet you'd like to know!'

'I want to know why she gave evidence against you.'

'Nah, she didn't! You don't know her – she's not like that.'

'Okay,' said Kuzak angrily. 'So why did she get up on the stand and screw you?'

'I've taken enough of this horseshit!' Carlton snarled. 'I need a bloody drink!' He started for the door.

Kuzak followed him. 'Is there another girl, maybe? Or does she have another guy?'

Carlton was standing almost next to Kuzak when he hit him. Kuzak, in a millisecond, saw the blow coming. He twisted round and rolled with the punch, which landed on the side of his head. He turned round and feinted with his right, then hit Carlton, twice, with his left, low down on the rib-cage. Carlton gasped with the pain and began to double up.

Kuzak stood over him, in case he tried to counter-attack, and thought, *This is bloody marvellous! I'm cited for contempt of court in the afternoon, and I assault my client in the evening!*

Carlton was sunk down against the desk, breathing in short hissing noises. 'You bastard. I'm hurt.'

At that moment the door opened and Ann Kelsey marched in. She stopped abruptly at the sight of Carlton. 'What on earth . . . ? Mike, what happened?' She remembered Markowitz's coronary here in the office, and thought the same thing was happening to Carlton.

'I got a little fresh with the client. That's all.'

'*That's all?*' She looked at him with wide-eyed horror. 'Michael, are you out of your mind?'

Carlton was trying to crawl to his feet. 'It's okay, ma'am – it was a fair fight. And I started it.'

'Jesus! Mike, this had better not get out. If Leland McKenzie hears, you're out on your ass!'

'It's all right, I won't be filing charges . . .' Carlton winced from the pain of speaking. 'I'd be glad if somebody would call me a cab.' He turned to Kuzak. 'Thanks for the hospitality, buddy-boy! But all good things come to an end.' He turned at the door. 'I'll call round tomorrow to get my gear.'

'What are you going to do now?' Ann said to Carlton.

'Right now, lady, I'm going to buy a bottle of Scotch and get well and truly smashed!'

Ann said to Kuzak, 'Ask Roxanne to call him a cab.' She turned back to Kuzak, her face livid with rage. 'God, Mike, sometimes I think you're still a kid!'

'Okay, Ann. From now on I'll practise turning the other cheek.'

'Did he really hit you first?'

'Yep. He's a boy with a lot of anxieties.'

'Is that why he hit you?'

'In a roundabout way, yes. His long-time girlfriend got on the stand today and did pretty bad . . . about as bad as you can imagine.'

'Hostile witness!'

''Fraid so. I was trying to get him to tell me what was wrong – and that's when he slugged me.'

She said, 'I think it would be a good idea, Mike, to run a trace on Doctor Janice Rhodes, of the San Fernando Clinic.'

'What d'you think you'll find?'

'Probably nothing. But at least we'll *know* there's nothing.'

133

'And your nice friend, Chuck Carlton? Are you still going to represent him?'

Kuzak frowned. 'I dunno. Fact is, I feel a little sorry for him. In just ten days it seems the whole world's turned against him. In fact, I'm not so sure I wouldn't have taken a slug at someone, in the same circumstances.'

She smiled. 'That's because you're a heroic idealist. No, no, I mean it, Mike! Carlton doesn't deserve you. We might as well run a trace on Carlton, too. I just hope we turn up something helpful.' She blew him a kiss and went out.

Chapter Seventeen

Outside, the evening smog had combined with a thin brown drizzle, reducing the traffic flow to a crawl.

Carlton decided that this must be the worst day of his life. A drink was not only called for – it was mandatory. He told the Hispanic driver to take him downtown, to 'The Maze' – a famous watering hole for 'resting' thespians and out-of-work models and 'artistes', all trying to catch the eye of a talent-spotter or director. Carlton reasoned that the place was so full of people wanting to be noticed, they wouldn't have time to notice anyone themselves. On the few occasions he'd been there, he'd usually been taken for an actor himself. He just prayed his luck would hold and that no-one recognised him from that ghastly clip of him laughing outside the court.

He put on his dark glasses and smoothed down his

hair. No reason not to look his best, he thought – which reminded him that he'd left his ivory badger shaving-brush, and a pair of ivory-backed hairbrushes back at Kuzak's beach house. He thought, If any of those girls from McKenzie Brackman found out and got their hands on them, they'd probably destroy them – all in the great crusade against killing elephants and badgers for profit . . .

'You an actor, mister?' the driver asked, flashing his teeth in the mirror.

'Yeah, well sort of.' He got his cigarettes out and was about to light up when the driver said, 'Sorry, mister, no smoking . . .'

Carlton felt himself winding up for a row. But he was without wheels, in a city without pedestrians, where money, sodomy and safe sex were fine, and booze and cigarettes were close to being capital offences.

He didn't want to walk – tonight of all nights. To have the cops pick him up for vagrancy . . . ! After what had happened today, anything seemed possible. And the more he thought about it, the more horrible it all seemed . . . The furious little judge, then Kuzak storming out, down into the seething crowds at the bottom of the steps. And to cap it all, the whole ghastly episode neatly encapsulated on the evening's peak-time TV.

God I feel tired, he thought, I could sleep for a year. Got some pills at home – the ones Janice had been prescribed last summer when she'd been having her anxieties. Just two, on top of two whiskies, then he'd try to call Janice . . . He also had to call Simbel – find

136

out how he'd taken the evening news bulletin. It was bad all round – he knew that. He just wanted someone to hold. Someone to hold him.

Hell, he was in the big time! He earned lots of money, he was good-looking, he had a nice house . . . A beautiful girl. He scratched his stubble. Maybe young Kuzak had something there, thinking there was a mystery about the way she'd behaved in court today? The trouble was, where girls were concerned, Carlton was so egocentric, so deeply subjective in his relationships, that he often totally missed the storm-signals.

The cab had stopped outside 'The Maze'. The meter said $10.60 cents. Carlton gave the driver one ten and two one-dollar bills. The driver said, 'Fifteen dollars, sir.'

Carlton said, 'Meter says ten-sixty. I'm being generous. Okay?'

'No okay, now is night-rate. You can check.'

'Sure.' Carlton again felt an enormous weariness coming over him. This was a perfect way to end this most terrible of all days – to get into a fight with a wet-back cab driver who was trying to rook him of less than five dollars.

He got out two more dollar bills and said, 'Fuck you, Romeo!'

'Hey fuck you too, you gay bastard!'

Carlton smiled and waved good-bye to him. He wondered what the guy would think if he knew all of Carlton's problems?

'The Maze' was already packed with dizzy-looking

blondes and Joan Collins lookalikes and muscle-bound young men with deep tans, trying very hard to double as Arnold Schwarzenegger. Everyone was drinking and talking and looking, and nobody was listening. This suited Carlton, who was heartened by the unreality of the place.

At the bar he kept his head down, trying to avoid all eye-contact. He ordered a Manhattan – a whisky-sour without too much ice.

The barman, who had wet hair and very long eye-lashes, smiled and said, 'Do you prefer any particular brand of whisky, sir?'

'Chivas,' he said, deliberately mumbling; and in a wild moment he thought of confiding in the man – telling him everything, on the assumption that a gay barman at the hub of Tinsel-Town would at least have a fresh perspective on things. Less censorious, too. Like the hippy at dawn in Beverly Hills. And again he drew a complicated comfort from the memory of the hippy. Then he realised why. He *envied* the hippy, just as he was beginning to envy the gay barman, who now brought him his drink, smiling from under his eye-lashes, in an astonishing take-off of Mae West. 'Hope that puts some lead in your pencil!'

A very tall swarthy man, who was a dead ringer for Simon Bolivar on the cigar boxes, said in a rich Castillian accent, 'Will you be eating dinner, sir?'

'Nah, just drinking.'

'*Muy buen, señor.*' He bowed low and turned on the heels of his beautiful black calf-skin knee-boots.

Carlton looked in the long mirror behind the bar. He

138

decided he didn't look too bad. So what the hell! –
why let the bastards get me down? He drank half his
cocktail, then called the pretty boy and asked for a cold
beer.

He drank two, in quick succession, then finished his
Manhattan and asked for another.

He was thinking more clearly now. He was less tense.
Beginning to see everything in a new perspective –
re-examining the parameters of all his relationships! –
and he grinned to himself, as he pushed over his cocktail glass for a refill.

He looked round furtively at the crowded tables, the
crush along the bar, and was reminded of peacocks
preening themselves, each determined to impress, to
be admired, with the desperate optimism of people
eternally on the threshold of paradise. Tonight. Tonight
will be different . . .

Carlton was reassured to see that no-one was paying
him any special attention. Halfway through his third
Manhattan he suddenly felt happy. *Why the hell hadn't
he thought of doing this before? After that ghastly court,
why hadn't he just disappeared into a nice cosy bar and
relaxed?* What damned use was it going back to Kuzak's
office? Pious bloody lawyers! – oozing ethics and self-
righteousness. He'd show them! He didn't need a
lawyer. He was innocent. He'd go into court next week
and defend himself. What use was Kuzak? Kuzak had
screwed up – got himself cited for contempt of
court . . .

He signalled the barman for another drink. And
this time, when he turned to survey the room, he

experienced a sense of lightness, of release, of being *out of the shadow of the Valley of Death* . . .

There was a girl coming towards him, tall and curved, her body looking as though she were wrapped in cling-film. And suddenly, as he watched her, he became aware of an unpleasant sensation – an emptiness, a longing. Then he realised what it was. The girl had the same figure as Janice. He wanted her. He could feel his innards beginning to churn – to imagine what it would be like to lie again between sheets and smell, feel, taste . . .

Why had she changed? Kuzak had been right. Why had she behaved like that on the stand? Was she trying to hurt him – even destroy him? And now he felt a stab of panic. He wanted her, he wanted to pin her down, naked, and explode inside her!

Why had she changed? The crash – had that done it? The dead child – that was it. She worked all week with sick children, and instead of being hardened by suffer-ing, she'd grown doubly sensitive.

He called for another drink. He was happy now. He'd solved the conundrum – he knew why Janice had behaved as she did. *He* knew, while that jerk, Kuzak, didn't. Kuzak was a dumb lawyer. He, Carlton, would call up Simbel tomorrow and tell him that Kuzak was no damn good. He'd even punched Carlton on his bruised ribs . . . *Holy Moses!* Now that he could think about it clearly, he realised how monstrously Kuzak had behaved. It was outrageous! He'd sue the bastard. It wouldn't go to court. No sir! Because as sure as he was Charles Averlaine Carlton, McKenzie Brackman would pay up in a hurry, just to keep their reputation.

Yeah, he'd sue them. And as soon as the cheque was cleared, he'd go and see Simbel and say he was taking a six month sabbatical. And he'd go to Europe. Take Janice. Take her to Venice – screw her between linen sheets, under a window overlooking the Giudecca . . . He was a hard man – he knew that. He was hard and talented, but he was tender too. He loved Janice, he decided, and finished his third cocktail.

He felt a hand on his shoulder. He turned and saw a tall thin man with blond hair that was not his own. 'Are you called Carlton?'

No Mister, no Sir. Just Carlton. 'Who wants to know?' he growled.

The man nodded. 'I saw you on TV tonight. You killed two people and your attorney screwed up. Crazy, huh? The next Governor even said the case was proof of how degenerate our society has become.'

'*Who, whaaaa?*' Carlton had trouble focusing. His hands felt clammy. 'Where d'you hear this?' he said, noticing that his glass was empty again.

'Oh it was all on TV. After the News. You were on the News, then Roz Acker had a spot, attacking the new generation of greedy, irresponsible young people who drink too much, and drive expensive cars, and have unstable relationships.'

'You remember all that?'

'Well, it's mostly the same speech each time. See, I work part-time on her election campaign. For the governorship.'

Carlton fixed him with a look of glazed horror. 'Who

141

the hell are you . . . ?' He found himself studying the man in the most minute way, noticing that his cheeks and chin were slightly raw with barber's rash.

Carlton checked his watch. He'd only been in here forty minutes, at the outside, yet he'd already been recognised – and by a perfect stranger.

'You got the wrong guy. Okay?' He signalled for the cheque and paid from a wad of fifty-dollar bills.

'I could have sworn . . .' the man said wonderingly.

Carlton struggled through the crush round the bar, walking carefully to the telephones, where he called a cab.

Chapter Eighteen

The first cab decided he didn't like the look of Carlton, who'd stumbled and fallen across the bonnet of a car, just as the cab stopped. This sobered him slightly. 'Negative discrimination!' he shouted at the driver, who was black.

Next time round he gave the doorman a twenty-dollar bill, if he could get him a cab to take him to Sepulveda Drive. The next driver was bull-necked, with a broken nose and a thick East European accent. 'You very drunk, yes?'

'Yes,' said Carlton, and flashed his most beguiling smile, which came out more as a lopsided leer. And before the driver could say No, gave him another twenty-dollar bill. Then he repeated his address and slumped into the back. The cab turned north along Santa Monica.

'I'm an actor,' Carlton said, by way of short-circuiting any small talk.

'Oh yeah? You Robert Redford?'

Carlton found this extraordinarily funny. He sat forward and slapped the driver hard on the shoulder. The driver, thinking he was being assaulted, slammed on his brakes and the cab went into a terrifying skid on the wet road, ending up facing back the way they had come, but on the wrong side of the road.

'You get out of my fuckin' cab! Or I get police!'

Carlton clambered out, smoothing down his hair and crumpled suit. 'I meant no harm, friend. No harm at all!' A car drove past, hooting and sending up a great curtain of spray that soaked him to the knees.

And in the same moment, just as the cab was trying to do a U-turn into the oncoming traffic, an alarm bell started to sound in the deepest recesses of his brain; he was alone in an unfamiliar part of the city, in pouring rain, wearing an expensive suit, carrying a fat wallet, drunk and there for the taking. L.A. wouldn't live up to its reputation if he wasn't at least mugged.

He lurched round to the front of the cab, waving his wallet. The driver slowed. Carlton had a fifty-dollar bill in his hand, then another. 'One hundred bucks, for Chrissake, just to Sepulveda Drive! *Please!*'

The driver took the money and told him to get in. Carlton did so, and suddenly felt very wet and very cold, and almost sober. He peered over the driver's shoulder and read the man's name on the identification disc on the windshield.

'Thank you – Mr Khatharchurian! You are a good man – and I salute you.'

'You have too much to drink.' The man's voice was heavy and monotonous.

'I have had a very terrible day,' Carlton said, imitating the driver's lugubrious tone. 'I have been to the brink and looked over it.'

'You should not drink unless it is a wedding, or a very important occasion.'

'But good sir, the girl I love has turned her back. She is in hiding. I think she does not love me any more.'

'Maybe she no like you drinking. Women and drink, they are not so good. Together, I mean.' And Carlton saw him crack a tentative smile in the driving mirror.

'Ten days ago I smashed my car. Brand-new – BMW, German car. Know it?'

'Of course. It is very expensive.'

'First day I had it, I went for a drive with my girl up past Bel Air and West Hollywood, and *wham*! I drove straight into another car. Both cars – totally wrecked. Tragic, huh?'

He watched in the mirror to see the driver's reactions. Had he watched the early TV bulletin? And would he now associate it with Carlton's face?

'For me, I lose my car, I lose everything. Until it is mended or I buy a new one.'

Carlton drew vicarious comfort from this exchange; he had practically confessed to the man, and there hadn't been a flicker of response. He decided to push harder. 'You ever been in a bad crash, Mr Khatharchurian? I mean, one where someone was killed?'

145

The driver looked suspiciously up at him in the mirror. 'Why you wanna know, huh?'

'Well – you know – I mean, I just wanted to know what the procedure was. Police procedure.'

'*Police!* Why you talk about police?'

'Just that I got this friend who was in a crash –' He hesitated, trying to unscramble his befuddled brain. '– He thinks he's in a jam. He wonders what'll happen? He's anxious about the police, the procedures – y'know . . . ?'

The driver's face was blank. Carlton decided that the man was not going to unburden himself after all, and had slumped back again into the seat, when the driver started talking:

'Yeah, well I know this cab driver what operates out of Sunset. He work for a syndicate. He owns half the cab, the syndicate own the other half. Then he go knock down an old lady that's crossing on the WALK sign. But he said she started walking when it showed DONT WALK.'

'What happened?' Carlton leant forward eagerly, his antennae quivering with expectation. Even at a hundred bucks, this was cheap at the price.

'What happened?' repeated the driver. 'Yah well not so good, huh. I mean, there's an Inquiry, see, because the lady she dies in the hospital, and he gets – how dya say?'

'Indicted?'

'Yeah, indicted. They call it "involuntary manslaughter" and he has to raise two thousand bucks for bail. So he don't have more than five hundred bucks, so he sells his share in the cab, but for that he only gets twelve hundred bucks, because it's an old Chevy and he's told he's lucky with that.'

'What happened to the other three hundred bucks?' Carlton asked. He was feeling almost sober now.

'Yah well' – the driver stuck a finger in his ear and rotated it, as though to stimulate his memory. 'The rest of the cabbies, we went round to get the donations, but we could only raise about eighty. He was a mean guy and nobody much liked him.'

'Did he have a lawyer – someone who could get the bail lowered?'

'Yeah, he had a lawyer but the guy went to the wrong court. By the time he showed up, the cabbie was in jail.'

'What happened in the end?' Carlton asked excitedly. This was better than just legal advice, it had all the makings of raw drama.

Again the cabbie took his time answering. He seemed to be admiring the houses behind their well-tended ornamental gardens on Sepulveda Drive. 'Very nice places, very quiet – nice play to live, huh?'

Carlton told him where his house was, about a quarter of a mile ahead. He said, 'So what happened to the cabbie in the end?'

'Well not so good. He was from Puerto Rico, so he thought maybe there was some prejudice when they didn't lower the bail, and didn't let him keep his cab. So to get him out o' jail, his wife took out a loan – you know?'

'Loan-shark,' Carlton said helpfully.

147

'Yeah, that's it. Fuckin' Korean guy. And by the time the case is about to start, the wife owes this bastard more than a thousand bucks! Howd'ya like that?'

'But didn't the lawyer do anything to help?'

'Nah, he was too late. Night before, the guy go take a whole bottle o' pills and a bottle o' whisky, and in the morning all they got to try is a stiff.'

For the last few hundred yards they drove in silence. As the cab drew up outside his miniature Spanish castle, he peeled off another fifty from his wallet.

The driver nodded. 'You take it easy, huh? This city's all full o' bread lice.'

As the cab drove away, Carlton wondered what bread lice were, or whether he'd heard right. Certainly for a hundred and fifty bucks, it hadn't turned out to be quite the advice he'd have wanted. In fact, the driver's tale had cast him suddenly into the slough of despond. He unlocked the three patent locks, plus the deadlock, and went into his house. He wondered what the Last Hippy was up to? Where he went at night, and when it rained?

*

It was still only just after ten o'clock. He surveyed his house with proprietorial pleasure. It was a nice house, the acme of a bachelor residence, comfortable but spartan, with only a few pots of make-up and a couple of

148

pairs of high-heeled shoes to connect him with Janice.

He began to think about Janice. When he had taken possession of the car, and had just won the Praxel account for the agency, he had been too cock-a-hoop, too damned over-confident that he had barely considered what Janice might be feeling or thinking, or what she needed or wanted.

She was a beautiful girl, although a somewhat passive one. She had a wonderful body. Carlton could honestly say that he had never met a girl who quite came up to her standard. He often told her this, confirming his feelings with erotic triumphalism – a phrase she had picked up at her aerobics class. Actually, from time to time she used some damned silly phrases. Came with living in California. She came from Flagstaff, Arizona, and often expressed the urge to return.

Carlton treated her – to some extent, deliberately – as a prized possession. And while still prizing her, he had noticed in recent months she was showing traces of discontent, even rebellion. At the Rackets Club on Sunset he had taken to dismissing her coolness with the phrase, 'the natives are growing restless'. To her face he said nothing, although he had noticed over the past two months that she was often moody and depressed, as often as not seemed unwilling to go to bed with him, and when she did, it was with a kind of weary resignation.

He considered her now as he undressed and waited for the green marble jacuzzi to fill. He wanted her, and wanted to call her, but something inhibited him. The same thing, perhaps, that made him unwilling to run through his messages on the answering machine, and had left the stack of mail untouched in the box.

He wondered where she was staying? Had she gone back to Bear Lake? Or was she at her apartment in Pasadena? It was easy enough to call her. Yet he didn't want to. He realised, with a slight chill, as he lowered himself into the tepid bubbling water, that the reason was simple enough. It was because she would turn him down. He didn't think of it in terms of betrayal, but that's in fact what it was. Her performance in court today was just that – cold-blooded treachery. But why? It was almost as though she had signed a pact with that boor Sharkey and that wretched McIvor man.

Hell's bells! he thought. I've got to get things sorted out. The insurance on the car – a new lawyer – maybe even a new girl. In this city they came a dime a dozen. And he was a superb catch, he tirelessly reminded himself; he was only just into his thirties, he had a fine profile, an elegant head of hair, and he earned a minimum of $120,000 a year, depending on commission. With the Praxel account he'd go into orbit!

He turned up the thermostat on the jacuzzi. He felt cold. Perhaps he'd caught a chill in the rain. He tried to relax, lie still, drift into a quiet trance. It was something that Janice could do, almost effortlessly. Last summer they'd driven to Northern California, beyond San Francisco, and gone on an orgy of 'hot-tubbing' where she'd lain naked and barely conscious of life round her. When he'd made love to her afterwards, she was warm and soft but curiously without passion.

To hell with her! He was getting a hard-on just thinking about her! So why couldn't he just call her up? She had her own car. If she were home, at this hour, she could be here in fifteen minutes.

But he wouldn't call, not only because he knew she would refuse, but also because she would know he had been drinking. And Janice knew all the signs, all the tricks. She had once said, with clinical detachment, that one of the most unpleasant things she had never experienced was going to bed with a drunk man. It was not just the body-odour and the flaccid incompetence, it was the puffy, screw-eyed face, the gibbering stupidity, the thought of a body poisoned with toxic waste.

Goddammit! He lumbered out of the jacuzzi and into a cold shower. She was fundamentally a prude. A nice country girl who looked after sick children. A nice, beautiful prude. Perhaps the last sexy prude in California? Or perhaps she was a portent of things to come?

Carlton towelled himself down and put on a silk kimono – the one Janice had given him five summers ago when they'd first met – and lay down on a bamboo *chaise longue*, feeling tired and extremely depressed.

I gotta get myself out of this! he thought. *I've gone right down. Rock-bottom. Can't go anywhere except up. I gotta get into bed. Sleep it off.*

He found the sleeping-pills that Janice had been prescribed in the summer; there were five left. He took three, reckoning that his resistance to alcohol would also lessen the effect of a normal dose of one or two.

Then he drank a litre of water, to neutralise the dehydration, and went to bed, waiting for the sleeping-pills to act. He tried not to think about Janice.

151

The awful thought occurred to him – had been occurring to him in one way or another all evening – that he might never again experience the sublime ecstasy of going to bed with Janice Rhodes.

He felt a stab of panic. But he knew he'd done the right thing. He hadn't called her. And in the morning it would all be different. Tomorrow he'd have nothing to drink. One day at a time. Then, to use her expression, *he'd re-examine the parameters of their relationship.* Smiling to himself, he drifted into heavy sleep.

Chapter Nineteen

Kenneth Clipner already had that feeling that the tide
was not running in his client's favour. The expression
'laughed out of court' might have been invented for
the case of Lowens vs. America's Most Embarrassing
Practical Jokes. For the fact that not only the plaintiff's attorney, Victor Sifuentes, but also the judge,
had been creasing themselves with laughter throughout the hearing might indicate, to an impartial
observer, that Professor Lowens was not getting a
fair deal.

For how the hell can you dispense justice if you can't
even keep a straight face? To make matters worse,
while everyone else was laughing, poor Lowens had
sunk, almost literally, into deep despair. He had not
only lost a good job, he'd now almost entirely lost his
self-respect. How can you respect a man who has his

wig lifted off on TV? It was worse than being a clown. At least clowns are *paid* to be funny, while the wretched professor was paid to be deadly serious.

It was nearly noon, which is the sleepy hour in L.A., even with the air-conditioners humming throughout the building, like the engines of a great ship. Los Angeles County Court, Room Three, was host to one of the best shows in town – providing you didn't have to pick up the tab at the end of the proceedings.

Attorney Kenneth Clipner had on the stand a handsome, well-groomed blonde in a power-suit, padded shoulders like a football player, and a diamond pin in her hair like a dagger. Watching her, Victor Sifuentes decided that for sheer, masculine aggression and ruthlessness, no-one – male or female – could rival Mrs Gail Eagan, the producer of America's Most Embarrassing Practical Jokes.

In comparison to his client, Clipner looked a trifle *under-powered* with his Ronald Colman moustache and snappy little polka-dot tie. When he went into battle on her behalf, he gave the impression of an old-fashioned gangster's sidekick playing at being tough. Today, he had no need to rehearse his witness – Gail Eagan knew her lines by heart:

'Professor Lowens signed the release. We were therefore fully authorised to air the tape.'

Clipner said, with more than just a trace of sarcasm, 'Of course, Professor Lowens claims he didn't know what you'd done.'

'Well, we're certainly very sorry for the misunderstanding. But believe me, we'd never put anything on our show without the full consent of all the participants. And here we had it.'

Clipner gave an ingratiating bow. 'Thank you, Mrs Eagan. Nothing further.'

Sifuentes stood up and eyed her thoroughly, as though measuring her for a suit. 'Mrs Eagan, did you bother to show my client this tape before airing it?'

'No, we don't do that.'

Sifuentes nodded. 'You don't do that, huh? And my client had no reason to know that you'd be putting in those little sound effects?'

Gail Eagan stiffened, as though her honour were being questioned. 'Those are creative choices we make in post-production. We –' she began – but Sifuentes was in there like a cat after the cream.

'The truth is, Mrs Eagan, you profit out of other people's misery, do you not?'

He saw at once that he had touched a raw nerve. The elegant veneer cracked, and her voice became as refined as a bucket of cement.

'Listen to the nice lawyer here, who takes train wrecks on a contingency –'

Sifuentes was on his feet, shouting, 'Objection! Move to strike that . . . !' It was getting to be personal now, as Mrs Gail Eagan taunted him:

'You don't ever profit off people's misery, do you, Mr Attorney?'

'We don't willingly *inflict* it!'

Judge Lang chuckled with appreciation. 'Good shot!'

Mrs Eagan stood with shoulders squared, her face

taut with rage. 'No, you're all here to make the world a better place.'

'Objection,' said Sifuentes, almost as a reflex.

'All right,' said Judge Lang. 'Touches all round. Now let's go.'

Sifuentes turned and faced the stand, as if to tell Mrs Eagan that the dislike was mutual.

'Mrs Eagan, I wonder why someone like you would want to pull off a man's hairpiece and embarrass him like that?'

'Again we thought he okayed it.'

'Well, would you yank the false teeth from the mouth of a senior citizen? Or pull the prosthesis off an amputee?'

'Of course not.' She looked at Sifuentes with contempt.

'Why of course not?'

'Because that wouldn't be funny.'

Sifuentes nodded. 'But it's funny to victimise this man?'

'Well, the judge laughed!'

Sifuentes turned and allowed his gaze to pass over the jury, before returning to Mrs Gail Eagan on the stand. 'This television show of yours makes a lot of money airing this kind of material, doesn't it?'

'We were fortunate to get a good time slot and –'

'You make *a lot of money*!'

'Yes, we do.'

Sifuentes smiled inwardly. He could see that he'd hurt her, had cracked that fearsome exterior. 'As an executive producer of this top-ten show,' he said, 'how much do you *personally* make?'

Clipner jumped to his feet, with a fair imitation of outrage on behalf of his client. 'Objection!'

'Overruled,' said Judge Lang. He looked as though he were enjoying himself.

Sifuentes closed in for the kill. '*How much?*'

'I make forty-five thousand per episode.'

Sifuentes nodded. 'You got paid forty-five thousand dollars to have his hair go up like a rocket.'

Gail Eagan flinched. She looked trapped. 'Not just for that,' she said, rather desperately. 'There were three other gags. There was the fat lady . . .'

'The point is, Mrs Eagan –'

'. . . the fat lady who tripped over the midget,' she went on, knowing she were outgunned.

Sifuentes' voice grew to a crescendo. 'The point is, *you* got rich and Professor Lowens lost his job. Right?'

'We're sorry about that,' she said, as though she'd done nothing worse than tread on Lowens' toe.

'You're sorry about that!' He gave her a withering glare, then turned to the judge. 'Nothing further.' And he returned to his seat.

*

'Looks like our boy fell at the first fence.'

Arthur Simbel stood with his back to the wide copper-tinted window overlooking the sweep of Pacific Palisades. It was like being on the bridge of an ocean liner, and he was the Captain. He was the boss. He

157

made the rules in the office, and he expected to be obeyed. But he also wanted to be seen as humane.

Tough but tender was his slogan; you don't get the best out of your workers if you flog them.

'Don't like doing it,' he said: 'Not one bit. Not one little itsy-bitsy.'

He looked down the long conference table at his Creative Director, Joe Glow, a stocky young man with dyed-white, shoulder-length hair and big pink spectacles. He was busy picking his teeth with a silver pick.

'I blame myself, in a way,' Simbel droned on, desperate for reassurance. 'That's why I retained McKenzie Brackman to represent him. I wanted him looked after, and they're supposed to be good. The best.'

'All lawyers are schmucks,' the Creative Director said, examining the pick for traces of blood.

'It's just too goddam awful! The crash . . . the publicity . . . having him off work, hiding at his lawyer's like some fugitive. And then last night . . . I feel kinda sick just thinking about it . . . It wasn't just seeing him on TV – it was the *context* that was so awful! What in heaven's name induced him to be filmed *laughing*?'

'Nervous reaction maybe?'

'But that's why I got him a good lawyer. 'Least I thought he was a good lawyer.'

'A schmuck, like I said.' Joe Glow yawned. Personally, he didn't give a damn about Chuck Carlton. He knew why Simbel kept him aboard – it was what he called the 'Ivy League' streak, the touch of class that

Carlton brought to his work. That was the reason why he had been upfront all along while they were clinching the Praxel deal. While sharp, vulgar brutes like Joe Glow laboured hard and long at the coal-face, the smoothies like Charles Carlton wined and dined and celebrated a famous victory . . .

Arthur Simbel looked pained. He felt cheated and confused. He needed to convince himself as much as his Creative Director. 'I talked to the lawyer last night. He implied that he was unhappy about Carlton – about the way things were going. *Goddam it!* I'm not paying him to like Carlton – I'm paying to keep his and our noses out of the shit!'

He stared unhappily down the table. 'What d'you think, Joe? What do I do? Put him on ice? Sabbatical? Wait till it all blows over?'

'So? Think it will blow over? With that cookie feminist running for the next Governorship . . . ?'

'She won't win,' said Simbel indignantly. 'Californians may be crazy, but not *that* crazy!'

'Okay. But the lady gets a lot of free air-time. She makes a lotta speeches, she makes lots o' waves. If she does nothing else in this campaign, she'll sink Carlton, and us with him – unless you let him go.'

Simbel looked wretched. It all seemed so sleazy and unfair. And what if Carlton tried to sue for wrongful dismissal? The publicity for that might be even worse. 'I just feel bad about treating him like he was already guilty. I hate it.'.

'So what'ya gonna do? Lose the Praxel account? And maybe a few others too?'

'But he has *not yet* been found guilty!' Simbel repeated, with anger this time, arguing with himself as much as with his Creative Director.

Joe Glow yawned again. 'Point is, Arthur, handsome Harvard Boy has screwed up – and mightily. He's been smeared all over the newspapers and paraded on television, and the Praxel people will have seen it, and they won't have liked it.'

'They can't pull out at this stage. They've *signed*, for Chrissake!'

'They can pull out all right. They'll find a way. People like us don't argue with people like Praxel. They call the shots. And they won't like having their good name associated with our Harvard Boy.'

'Carlton's a good copywriter . . .'

'Sure. This city's full of good copywriters who can hold their liquor and don't kill children with their cars.' Joe Glow placed his stubby index finger, with its thick gold signet ring, against the middle of his forehead, letting out a low, slow wailing sound, like some mystic incantation.

Arthur Simbel gaped at him. He knew Glow smoked dope, but he wondered now if he tried something stronger. The wailing noise went on; the Creative Director seemed to be enjoying himself. He stopped suddenly, smiling.

'The Evil Eye. Like Napoleon said – we don't need good ad men – we need lucky ones. And oh boy! our Boy Carlton is lucky like Saddam Hussein was a great general! Carlton is a *disaster*, Arthur! Put him over the side.'

'And Praxel? Not to mention the other clients he's been working with?'

'You let it get around that Carlton's had the bullet, and they'll forget him. But just make sure you do it before they start wondering why Simbel & Horne retains a semi-alcoholic child-killer as their star turn!'

'You don't like him, do you, Joe?'

'Like milkshakes – I don't like 'em, I don't dislike 'em. Just don't care for the flavour.'

Arthur Simbel folded his hands across his stomach and said stiffly, 'Thanks for your advice, Joe. Now I'd better go and make some calls.'

Chapter Twenty

'If the only trouble you got, Victor, is a guy who gets his wig lifted off before twenty million people, then you don't know what trouble is.' Kuzak was pacing the conference room, twelve steps one way, twelve steps back.

Ann Kelsey said, 'You're getting too involved, Mike. You're too sympathetic to him. We're not one of the caring professions. We're in the business of getting results according to the law. We work the law, like a sculptor works a hunk of marble . . .'

'Hey! Hey! Hey!' Arnie Becker cried. 'Tie me down! My feet are leaving the ground.'

Markowitz sat frowning, like a very wise mole. 'If what you say is true, he is no longer strictly speaking our client.' He looked at Brackman for guidance.

'I guess that's true,' Brackman said, 'insofar as it

was Arthur Simbel who initially hired us to look after Carlton's interests.'

'Which we did absolutely *magnificently*!' Kuzak said, keeping up his restless pacing.

'You mean, *you* did absolutely,' Becker said. 'The rest of us had nothing to do with the man.'

'Sounds like you don't like him?' said Kuzak.

'I got no feelings at all about him. I don't *know* the guy. You're the expert on Mr Chuck Carlton. Why, you've had him under wraps, all snug as a bug in a rug, for going on ten days. More to the point, Mike – *D'you* like him?'

'Look, he's not a saint.' Kuzak looked nervously at Ann Kelsey, wondering how long he could keep their recent fisticuffs a secret. 'He's just a regular guy who's got himself in a jam. Okay?'

From the head of the table Leland McKenzie spoke with the muted authority of a founding partner. 'I'd be happier if you'd sit down.' He waited while Kuzak resumed his seat. 'What you're really saying, Mike, is that your client has been set up – that he's become a very useful pawn in certain people's personal and political ambitions?'

'Bulls-eye!' said Kuzak.

'Only it's difficult to prove? Yes?'

'Leland, I watched that TV election-spot last night a dozen times. Roz Acker is no fool. She didn't mention Carlton *by name*. But she mentioned just about everything else about him. If there are people who still don't make the connection, by the time we get to the new hearing, she'll have made damned certain that Chuck

163

Carlton's reputation is about on a par with the Boston Strangler. "Child-murderer" they're calling him – although not by name. Not yet.' He paused, took a deep breath. 'I tell you all, this is one of those cases that makes me feel ashamed of American Law.'

'Aw c'mon, Mike,' said Arnie Becker. 'This gonna turn into a crusade for truth?'

Kuzak looked at him with icy disdain. 'I think maybe there aren't enough crusades for the truth.'

Becker lifted his hands in a gesture of mock surrender. 'Me, I'm just a mean old lawyer in a mean old town called L.A. How did I ever think I was anything else?'

Leland McKenzie turned to Brackman. 'I think we ought to wrap this one up, Douglas. How far you got with Simbel?'

Brackman frowned. 'Fact is, Leland, Simbel wants out. Our brief was to keep his agency out of the spotlight. That we failed to do. So he's cashed in his chips and gone home.'

'And Carlton?'

'He says he intends to let Carlton go,' Brackman said.

'On what grounds?' said McKenzie. 'I thought he was a star performer with the agency? Got them the Praxel account and all that.'

'Yeah, well' – Brackman frowned hard at his reflection in the highly polished table. 'He did mention something about there being grounds of "moral turpitude" and thus embarrassing his clients.'

'Oh my God,' McKenzie said, 'I've not heard that

phrase – moral turpitude – since the Fifties! It went out with Joe McCarthy and the UAAC. Or does this city *want* to go back to those days?'

'The new wave of Puritanism,' Brackman said. 'See Roz Acker for Governor and the Reverend Weekes as Keeper of the Californian soul!'

Kuzak stood up noisily. The others looked at him. Abby said, 'Where are you going?'

'I'm going to find Chuck Carlton. I reckon he needs a lawyer.'

*

Carlton woke from a ten hour sleep. He showered and shaved and made himself a *cafetiere* of black coffee, sliced a half of grapefruit, and warmed up two croissants from the freezer.

Then he forced himself to play back his messages on the answering machine. There were about a dozen calls from newspapers and TV and radio stations. They all made it sound as though they wanted to do him a favour. A couple of them mentioned money.

He waited impatiently for the whirring, then the bleep . . . He wanted to hear Janice's voice. He wanted to be reassured, made to feel that he was not abandoned, was not alone . . . Yet his thick, arrogant, egocentric hide still prevented him from realising quite how weak and vulnerable his condition had become.

The insurance company had rung, and wanted him

to call back. That was two days ago. The last message, from yesterday, was Arthur Simbel's secretary, Miss Pym, asking him to come by the office as soon as possible. He frowned, and played the message again. Simbel usually rang him at home himself. Perhaps he'd been too busy – something to do with the Praxel account, maybe? For Praxel was Carlton's baby, and he wasn't going to let anyone forget it.

He didn't allow himself to worry too much about this. He'd call the office and make an appointment. Simbel had given him fourteen days' leave of absence, on full pay, and Carlton still had three days to run. It had been a fair precaution: nobody wanted the TV and Press camping out on the steps of Simbel and Horne, for Chrissake! But that was yesterday – more than yesterday, it was nearly ten days ago. And yesterday's news was about as exciting as watching two old men chewing tobacco.

What did worry him was that Janice hadn't rung. That was galling. She'd promised that if she went away again, she'd leave a message where he could reach her. Instead, nothing. Thus the click, then the whirring . . . as though into eternity; and listening to it reminded him of her blank stare on the stand yesterday, her voice almost too low to be heard.

He poured one more cup of black coffee, and repeated out-loud several times: 'I am not going to take a drink today.' Just for today. That's what's been happening, he thought – I've been getting out of condition, too much time drinking and screwing. Correction! – too much time drinking and drinking, and putting on his best Boston Brahmin accent to impress the clients. Correction! – *His* clients . . .

He called the office. 'Arthur Simbel, please.' A tiny silence, then Miss Pym came on the line. 'Yes . . . who shall I say is calling?'

'Tell him it's Clint Eastwood and that Arthur doesn't get killed till the last reel.'

She sucked in her breath and said, 'One moment please.'

Carlton finished his coffee, then carried the 'phone over to the mirror where he inspected his reflection for blemishes. He looked good. The sleep had ironed out the creases and hollows under his eyes, and the shower had brought a slight flush to his cheeks. Yep, he looked great. Simbel and Horne had every reason to feel proud having him on their payroll.

'Mr Carlton? – it *is* you, isn't it?' The secretary sounded a little huffy, as though he'd used a rude word.

'The one and only!'

'Mr Simbel would like you to come to the office as soon as possible.' And before he could question her further, she had rung off.

He was mildly annoyed. He didn't exactly expect to be treated as an equal by Simbel, but he most certainly did not like being fobbed off by some secretary.

Then he remembered – as he had done every morning for ten days now – that he didn't have a car. *Wheelless in L.A.*, he thought, like some mighty 20th Century epic. And he remembered Mike Kuzak had told them that the police had a file bulging with cases of guys who'd lost their licences and went out and killed themselves. Apparently, as a cause of suicide by men it was the second highest, after marriage break-up, and on a par with bankruptcy.

He called the nearest cab, on Wilshire, lit a cigarette and rinsed out the breakfast things. The little jingle on the front door sounded, just as he was about to light a second cigarette. And yet again he cursed the loss of his car. It made him feel like an amputee. A cripple. A man *couldn't exist* in this city without wheels. Might as well cut a man's balls off, he thought, turning the four locks and walking through the wrought-iron gates to the cab, where he could already see the smug little notice: *L.A. Thanks You for Not Smoking and Helping to Make This a Cleaner City.*

The driver looked like a Filippino and was tapping his fingers on the leopard-skin steering-wheel, listening to Madonna. Carlton got in and gave him the address in Pacific Palisades. 'You mind turning the music down a bit?'

Carlton saw the white teeth sneering at him, as the driver turned down the sound perhaps two decibels. Okay, he thought, and ostentatiously lit a cigarette.

The driver took no notice; and he and Carlton drove all the way to Pacific Palisades, listening to Madonna and filling the cab with a comforting blue fug of toxic fumes.

Chapter Twenty One

The cab dropped Carlton just before noon at the foot of the Piedmont Building, which was like a great copper and glass sword rising in triumph above Pacific Palisades. Simbel & Horne was somewhere near the middle of two long rows of names engraved on a huge slab of bronze.

Carlton rode up to the twenty-ninth floor, in one of the little glass bubbles that moved up and down the outside of the building, like drops of mercury in a thermometer. He was watching the tiny flecks of surf breaking on the rocks far, far away, when the lift soundlessly stopped. The door slid open, and Carlton was back in the saddle – the adman who had just about everything – except for his lovely car and a girl who didn't leave messages. And a little bit of legal hassle, of course. But he shrugged that off – it could wait its time.

The first thing that he noticed – though only in retrospect – was that Arthur Simbel's secretary, Miss Pym, sat with head lowered, pretending to go on with her touch-typing as soon as he appeared.

'Hello, gorgeous!' Carlton leered at her, his voice full of playful irony: for Miss Pym was what the Americans, with uncharacteristic tact, called 'homely'. 'Don't I get a kiss after ten days?'

He saw her neck flush; and she half-turned, still without looking at him, and said, 'I'll tell Mr Simbel you're here.'

Carlton gave her a good-humoured grin, and stood waiting, reminding himself that today saw the creation of the new Charles Carlton, adman extraordinaire, – indeed, Renaissance Man himself, in the heart of the City of Angels.

He felt relaxed, even light-headed. As he waited, he glanced through the half-open door into the engine-room of the agency: a long half-split room broken up into partitions, each fitted with daylight simulation bulbs where the creative personnel laboured over computers and drawing-boards and polystyrene models, or just doodled on block-pads with Bic pens.

He felt a moment of superiority. Not for him the sweat and toil of the creative room. From now on, with Praxel under his belt, he would be in the big time. As for the events of the past few days, that was merely an unfortunate blip on the upward curve . . . That was it! *A mere blip . . . the upward curve . . .* Trust him to come up with the *mot juste*.

He welcomed Miss Pym with a breezy smile. 'How is he? Snarling or purring?'

'He'll see you now,' she said, ducking down behind her desk. And Carlton reflected that only a firm of impeccable virtue could afford to exhibit secretaries of such deliberate lack of sex appeal.

He went through to what Simbel called The Bridge. Simbel himself stood framed against the window, while a second man was sitting at the table – a small greyish man with glasses, hands folded in front of him like napkins.

This was Harrison Glazetop Horne, the second partner in the firm of Simbel & Horne – soon, perhaps, with his triumphs still ringing across the West Coast, to grow into Simbel, Horne and Carlton. Chuck rolled the names on his tongue and round his mouth, as though tasting a fine wine. He decided, on mature reflection, that Simbel, *Carlton* & Horne sounded marginally better – more euphonic.

He came into the long sunlit room, smiling broadly, his body feeling cleansed and fit. Blinded by the great window he could not read any expression on Arthur Simbel's face; and his partner, Harrison Horne, who was by profession an accountant and managed the agency's finances, had about as much expression as a bar of soap.

'Hi Arthur, *ciao*! Mr Horne, sir, I'm honoured! We junior officers don't get enough opportunities to meet you Top Brass!' He beamed at the older man, calculating that a bit of healthy banter was quite in order when greeting his future equal. Horne acknowledged the remark with a very slight nod.

171

'Sit down, Chuck.' It was Simbel, pulling out a chair at the head of the table. Chuck did so, choosing a chair strategically mid-way between the two partners.

'Chuck, I've asked Harrison here to be in on this meeting in case there is the very smallest ground for misunderstanding.'

For a fraction of a second Carlton thought he saw the room darken; and he felt a slight heaviness in his legs. He stared at Simbel, who was still just a framed silhouette against the noon glare. He looked at Harrison Horne and remembered afterwards thinking how the little man's eyes looked like oysters behind his strong spectacles.

He turned again to Simbel. 'Sure, Arthur. Absolutely!' His mouth, with its strong jaw, dropped open and hung there in a vacuous grin. Feeling that the interview was not going quite as well as it should, he sat up and said, 'One must at all times minimise the dangers of misunderstanding – of a failure in communication. Absolutely.'

Carlton had a recurring dream, merging into nightmare, of standing on skis on what appeared to be a flat slope, then very slowly beginning to slide forward, gathering speed, yet at the same time powerless to move his limbs, try to turn or stop . . . Meanwhile, he hurtled on towards a chasm . . . What made the dream more sinister and destructive was the fact that skiing was one of Carlton's favourite sports, and one at which he excelled. Every winter he went to Purgatory, Colorado . . .

He felt his skis beginning to slide now, as he gave his

big handsome white smile. 'Hey you guys, it's great to be back in the saddle. Last ten days have been – er – just a blip on the upward curve . . .' He paused, still smiling. 'But I've sure gotten one piece of very good advice for you guys. Keep away from lawyers!'

Arthur Simbel cleared his throat, shuffled his hands, glanced at Harrison Horne, then said, 'I'm afraid I'm going to have to be frank with you, Chuck. We find ourselves in a very difficult situation. By "we" I mean the agency as a corporate entity. Now, normally I don't enquire too closely into our employees' private lives or what they get up to when they're not in the office. However' – the silence sang in Carlton's ears – 'there is one proviso to this. Publicity. And scandal.'

Carlton felt the skis beginning to race, his legs turning to jelly. The smile on his face was already turning into an agonised grimace, as he sat transfixed, listening to Arthur Simbel's low monotone.

'Now it may sound odd for an advertising agency to dread publicity. But as we in this profession all know, there is publicity *and publicity*.' He cleared his throat, choosing his next words with care:

'As you know, Chuck, my first priority after you'd been involved in the accident was to get you a good lawyer. However, things didn't pan out quite as we'd have liked. It seems that the publicity has been feeding on itself, until . . .' His words trailed off, as though he were somehow failing to convince himself, let alone the other two.

Carlton wanted to say something, but all that emerged was a thin groaning sound. He heard it with

173

a kind of mute horror, as if he'd just committed some sanitary outrage.

Arthur Simbel went on: 'Ironically, if it weren't for the Praxel account we might have been able to weather the storm. It was just bad timing. The Praxel people had gone back to Chicago, with the ink barely dry on the contract, when the TV and the papers were full of . . .' He flapped a hand, as though unable to find the words; instead, he looked for reassurance at Harrison Horne.

The little man spoke, barely moving his lips. 'It's unfortunate, Mr Carlton, but we have to think of the agency first. Above all else, the agency. That has to be our motto.' The grey oysters behind the spectacles moved from Carlton to Simbel, then back to Carlton. 'We are talking about what in politics is known as the "sleaze-factor" . . .'

It was at this point that Carlton's instinct for battle jolted him into speech.

'*Jesus H. Christ!* I don't believe what I'm hearing! You guys dare talk about the sleaze-factor! The sleaze-factor is the only goddam thing this city knows about! Just get out there and talk to people – not the big shots in the other agencies or the studios – just you get out there and talk to a few ordinary Joes – and you'll find that *everyone – every goddam one* – is doing his own little bit o' sleaze! – hustling and scamming and wheeling and dealing . . . ! You name it, they do it!'

Carlton paused, drew in his breath, then rose, with both fists clenched, and shouted, 'And you have the fucking gall to mention "sleaze" to me – *me* – Charles

Carlton, the one person who could bring a bit of class into this crummy hole in the floor – !'

'I refused to listen to any more of this!' said Harrison Horne, standing up and backing quickly to the door.

Simbel said quietly, 'I'm sorry it had to come to this. *Very sorry indeed.* You had a very big future in front of you, Chuck.'

'Arthur, don't be a pissing hypocrite! I know what happened. Before that woman who wants to be the State's next Governor was even off the air, you had Armitage and all the bank people at Praxel calling in and saying, *Nice copy. Pity about the creative director.* Right?'

'It wasn't as simple as that. I wish it had been. We might have been able to take a stand. It just happens that everyone – and I mean *everyone* who's anyone in L.A. – seems to have been watching TV that night and saw you laughing like a hyena, while the dead woman's husband – father of the kid,' – Simbel waved a hand as though trying to grab the right words – 'a five-year-old kid, Chuck – and you had to laugh in front of the whole West Coast. It was a shameful spectacle. Yet I did what I could to help you.'

'Yeah, you got me a lawyer. Bully for you! The guy got himself cited for contempt. Got any other favours up your sleeve?'

'I did what I could, Chuck. Believe me. I got that lawyer to try and take the heat off – to keep it nice 'n clean, outta the TV and everything. But it didn't work. And now that the politicians have got hold of it, it looks like it's one of those things that'll run and run.'

175

Carlton closed his eyes, tried to steady himself, the ground hurtling away from under him – the chasm racing up towards him. He said, half to himself, 'I thought I had it made. I thought I'd be up in lights – Simbel, Horne & Carlton . . .'

'Take it easy,' said Simbel. 'I'll see Accounts and get them make out a cheque for six months' salary.'

'*Six months!*' Carlton roared. 'I'd get more at a corner dime-store!'

'That may be so,' Simbel said, suddenly weary. 'Take it or leave it.'

Carlton sat as though frozen, waiting for the chasm to swallow him. He felt a surge of panic. He gasped, trying to get his breath back, to control the flood of words.

'Look, Arthur,' – he almost choked on the name – 'I got commitments. I got a house . . . a loan . . . mortgage repayments.'

'C'mon, Chuck – you're a lot luckier than some I've seen. You got no wife, no kids. You're lucky! We had a guy here once – before you came – who was past forty, and we had to let him go. He'd got about three loans, and everything in the house was in hock – but still we had to let him go. Know what he did? He got his car out – nice Chrysler convertible – and got a length of wire and fastened one end to the garage post and the other round his neck, then he started the car up and let out the clutch – *crack*! Like celery, one o' the cops said.'

Recounting this story seemed to have cheered Simbel

up; he even managed a smile. 'As they say, Chuck, worse things happen at sea!'

Carlton framed the words 'Such as?' but found his throat too dry. He swallowed and there was no saliva in his mouth. He saw Simbel coming round the table. 'You'll want an hour to collect your stuff, I expect?'

'You want me out in *an hour*?' he cried. Somehow, this upset him even more than getting fired. It was downright, deliberate humiliation. It was unlawful, he was sure of that. Get hold of young Kuzak, get him to take out a suit for unjustified dismissal, with aggravated circumstances. And thinking of Kuzak reminded him of something that he'd conveniently shovelled into the back recesses of his brain. *Kuzak had not told anyone about Carlton's assault on him.* That must be true, or Simbel would have thrown it at him first thing. Assaulting a high-class attorney who'd been appointed by his boss surely would qualify as the sleaze-factor. Yet Michael Kuzak had held his fire. Maybe he *was* a man of integrity. Hard to believe, but there it was.

He realised he had been standing immobile, staring in front of him, clenching and unclenching his fists, while Arthur Simbel had slipped noiselessly out of the room. Simbel was an asshole. They all were! He'd grab his cheque from Accounts and get the hell out of here. Call a few places and track down Jan, book two tickets to Europe. To hell with L.A. All the cliches were true: the city where everything looks like the road to the airport. Where sweat dries yellow, like urine.

He went through to his office. His name had been removed from the door, but had not been replaced. He stormed in and began casting round him, wondering where to start. Apart from reference books, a tennis racket and Reebok trainers, there was little of real value. Just then there was a tap on the door. A very pretty girl with wet shingled hair, white lipstick and a high, plump behind in skin-clinging jeans, smiled and said, 'Mr Carlton? Mr Simbel's secretary said you might need these.' And she handed him two large black plastic garbage-bags.

He stared at her, tried to smile back, and felt his nose and eyes brimming with tears. 'I haven't seen you before,' he said.

'I'm Arlene. I'm Mr Glow's new secretary.'

'Lucky old Mr Glow.' Vaguely he remembered hearing that Joe Glow was looking for someone. He boasted that he screwed every secretary he'd ever had within two weeks of being taken on, and that they usually lasted him six months.

Carlton looked at her as though she were some forbidden fruit. 'I got one hour to clear my desk and get out. D'you know all about it?'

'Yah, I heard something. I'm sorry.' She hesitated, and detected something in either his eyes or his posture that warned her off. He was a nice looking guy – the sort she usually went for – but just now he looked kinda weird, like he might go crazy any minute. She placed the bags on the desk and backed hurriedly out.

He thought of following her, showering her with C-notes, taking her up Beverly Hills and shopping with her – shopping so she could hardly walk, hardly stand! – then take her back to Sepulveda Drive. Would Jan suddenly arrive? The Press? The D.A.'s office? He felt hunted, claustrophobic, trapped in the chasm . . .

He ran out of the room, leaving the two black bags empty, and kept on running until he got to the elevators. A few minutes later he was outside, his eyes smarting with the heat. He went into a diner on the next block, ordered a black coffee and a sandwich, then rang for a cab.

Must get my act together – get myself a new car. Drive out of this motherin' mess! He was too absorbed by his accumulating misfortunes to notice a small blue European car, which had been parked half a block down the road with its engine running, now crawl forward and start following Carlton's cab.

Chapter Twenty Two

The trouble with laughing in a court of law is that it's like laughing in church. The solemnity of the occasion only magnifies the effect, until it generates a momentum of its own, which is easily triggered but not easily checked.

Judge Lang might have had this in mind, as he presided over the final stages of the case of Lowens vs. America's Most Embarrassing Practical Jokes.

'I hereby warn the court that any further displays of humour – any displays of *levity* or of a *jocular* nature, will not – I repeat, *not* – be tolerated by this court!'

Having made this portentious announcement, Judge Lang settled himself with his back half turned to the jury box, and a small impish grin playing around his mouth, as he prepared to enjoy Victor Sifuentes making his closing speech for the plaintiff.

'Your Honour – members of the jury – I ask you to pause a moment, to try and imagine yourselves in the shoes of my client. Imagine, if you will, the *shame* he must have felt that night as he sat and watched his hair just . . . hover above his head . . .' Sifuentes felt himself getting lock-jaw trying to keep his face in order.

'To be sitting at home, ladies and gentlemen, with your wife and kids, and to see it . . . see it go up to the sound of twin booster engines . . .' Here a giggle escaped Sifuentes' iron defences, but it escaped as a cross between a squelch and a snort. '. . . And the way it sputtered before it came crashing down . . .'

Here Sifuentes paused, his whole face frozen in an agony of immobility, squeezing out the words in a tight little voice that barely his own, knowing that once he lost control, and let slip the tiniest hint of a smile, all would be lost. To make matters worse, he knew that the jury were just waiting for him to smile first – like some hilarious version of who-blinks-first.

'My client was wronged, ladies and gentlemen,' Sifuentes declared, wondering how much longer he could keep this up. 'They snatched it right off with a fish-hook!' He turned and let out a little squeak of laughter, which was somehow worse than real laughter, because it revealed the true extent of his agony, as he tried doubling up and stuffing a handkerchief into his mouth.

The jurors took this squeak as a signal: several started to smile, then giggle, and a few creased themselves up in deep belly-laughs.

At this a small defiant voice was heard. 'Your Honour.' It was Professor Lowens.

Judge Lang looked down at him, far from pleased because the intervention placed him centre-stage, where he could be seen fighting his own battle to keep a straight face. 'Yes, Professor Lowens?'

'Your Honour, I would like to do my own closing.'

Sifuentes looked at the little man and said, in a slightly hoarse voice, 'I'll be okay – don't worry.'

'I would like to do it myself,' Lowens persisted.

The judge nodded. 'It's his right, Mr Sifuentes. Go ahead, sir.'

Sifuentes returned to his seat, exhausted by his unsuccessful exertions and not daring to make eye-contact with Lowens, who now approached the jury. He looked at them and smiled. 'It's okay to laugh.' And several of the jurors did so, rather guiltily.

'That's okay, really. I know that by wearing a toupee I hold myself up to that sort of thing. But the issue here is not whether my hairpiece is funny. Or whether the tape was funny – and we all know it was. Members of the jury, this is about respect. It's about people treating other people with respect.' There was a total hush in the courtroom. He had them all eating out of his hand.

'These shows – this one, the home video one – they all reward individuals for capturing the embarrassing misfortune of others. And people like me – we occasionally get caught up in it all. No matter how humourous it is, no matter how clever it is – it's disrespect. And if you've watched their show, you'll know that the more embarrassing it is, the more it *hurts* – then the funnier it is. We've just had proof of that, right here in court.'

He paused, dabbing a handkerchief to his brow. Sifuentes listened with a mixture of relief and faint shame. The little man was doing well.

Lowens continued. 'Members of the jury, when you go back to that jury room and laugh at me – I hope you'll remember that. That all the giggling and sniggering caused by these people has been at my expense. Thank you.' He gave a little bow and returned to his chair.

Judge Lang smiled down at him. 'Thank you, Professor. Admirably stated . . .'

*

The Jury were out for just under thirty minutes. They came in looking relaxed, almost as though they were enjoying themselves. The foreman rose, a powerfully built black in a three-piece suit and with distinguished grey hair like iron filings.

'In the matter of Lowens vs. America's Most Embarrassing Practical Jokes, we find in favour of the plaintiff, and order the defendant to pay damages in the amount of forty-five thousand dollars.'

'Thank you, ladies and gentlemen of the jury. This case is now adjourned.'

As the courtroom began to empty, Sifuentes walked up to Lowens, grinning rather sheepishly. 'Congratulations!'

'Thank you.'

'Look, Martin, I'm sorry.' – He fell in step beside Lowens – 'Well, I'm sorry I sort of laughed . . .'

'You don't have to apologise, Victor. It's surely *permissible* to laugh at bald people.'

'Maybe because society doesn't think it so bad to be bald. I mean, maybe we're insensitive to it because it's no big deal.'

Lowens just looked at him. Sifuentes felt embarrassed. 'It *is* no big deal, Martin.'

'You think I'm being silly?'

'I think you sued these TV people because you felt your dignity had been assaulted. But I also think' – Sifuentes groped for the right words – 'I think every time you put that thing on, well, it's like you're saying that you don't like yourself the way you are.'

Lowens gave a patient smile. 'You wear an earring, Victor – my wife likes her girdle – we all do what we do to make us look better. To make us *feel* better. Why can't the bald guy indulge himself like everyone else? I like myself just fine, Victor. I just like myself better with the hair. Okay?'

'Okay, Professor! Don't spend it all at once.' They shook hands and Sifuentes watched the little man lose himself in the throng of the courthouse atrium. One satisfied client, he thought. You didn't get one every day. Like Mike Kuzak. Jesus, he'd got the short straw and bombed!

Chapter Twenty Three

Inside his house, Carlton drank two cups of fresh black coffee, a pint of iced water, smoked a couple of cigarettes, then inspected his hands. They were almost steady; but his head was so full of contradictory emotions that he could only concentrate by sitting down and jotting out a list of priorities on a clipboard:

JANICE – Try Apt. then Clinic
LAWYER – find SOMEONE NEW. BRACKMAN,
ergo KUZAK in hock to Simbel
BANK – check balance, plus LOAN.
CAR – buy new one.
INSURANCE – answer message.

He stared moodily at the items, deciding which would be most rewarding, or the least painful. He pulled the phone over and dialled Janice's apartment. On the ninth ring he was greeted by his own voice – slow and commanding, he always thought – announcing that Dr Rhodes was not available . . . etc. (It had been his idea after yet another heavy-breathing freak was trying all numbers that answered with a female voice. As he remembered, the freak in question had turned out to be a 14-year-old drop-out from a private school in Bel Air. Ah, the delights of the City of Angels!)

He tried the number a second time, in case he'd caught her in the bath. Again, Chuck Carlton, with a voice to match his profile.

He rang the Clinic in Pasadena. A woman answered crisply, 'San Fernando Clinic for Children – can I help you?'

He tried offhand, and at the same time commanding, as he did on the answering tape. 'Yeah – I'd like to talk to Dr Janice Rhodes.'

There was a second's pause; and when she spoke next there was a faint wariness in the voice. 'Who is it calling, please?'

He thought, What the hell – a little bit of subterfuge. She'd understand: it was like the answering machine, only more so. What with all the publicity, newsmen camped out on her lawn, besieging the clinic. No wonder they were wary of callers.

'My name's' – he hardly paused – 'Arthur Simbel, of Simbel and Horne, the advertising agency. It's urgent that I speak to Dr Rhodes as soon as possible.'

'May I have your number, Mr Simbel, and I'll get her to call you.'

'Isn't she working at the clinic?'

'I'm sorry, sir, but we have instructions not to put through outside calls. But if you'd like to leave your number . . .'

He gave it – his home number. If she wanted to call, she'd call. If not, well . . . He was like the captain of a ship steering between rocks and submarines. Things were going to get worse before they got better. Ordeal by fire and water . . .

He waited on the little sun-trap which the realtor had described as a 'sunshine patio'. The sky was a steel glare and made him sweat almost at once. He went back inside, experiencing the nervous reality of being unemployed, of having to kill time while waiting for the phone to ring. And again he felt that small stab of panic that he'd felt at the end of his meeting with Simbel and Horne . . .

Renaissance Man, proud knight of the advertising industry, was on his own. If it had been of his own choosing, he'd have found it exciting, even exhilarating. He could start his own agency, maybe . . . When the case was over. And if some of the mud stuck – *Child-Killer Adman* – he could always move East, touch up his slight English accent and turn his charms on the Boston Brahmins. Cape Cod and the rich literary folk . . . Norman Mailer – he'd hardly blink at the Child-Killer myth. He might even take up Carlton's cause – a victim of the judicial system . . .

The phone rang. It was Janice.

'Jan, where the hell have you been? Look, I've been worried half sick.'

'I thought you didn't want to see me any more.'

'What made you think that? At the court I didn't want us both to get snared up with the media.'

'That was considerate of you.' (Just a trace of irony in her voice? he wondered.) 'But it didn't do any good, did it? We got ensnared – both of us.'

'Look, Jan – when can I see you?'

'Well, when . . . ?'

'Today. Now.'

There was a long silence. He thought they'd been cut off. 'Jan – you still there?'

'Yes, I'm still here. I'm off at six. You know the Brasserie near the Clinic . . . ?'

'Hey, that's down-market, honey! Why don't we go to a good restaurant – ?'

'No Chuck. We did that last time. It doesn't work. You don't have to impress me.'

'Okay.' He found himself frowning at his feet, suddenly lost for words. 'So we'll meet in the Brasserie – great!' he said, with artificial jollity. 'You name the time.'

'I won't have time to change. I'll see you at six-thirty. Okay? – must go now.'

He'd wanted to talk to her more, ask her more about her performance in court, but she'd hung up. In a funny, irritating way he felt cheated. Nothing and nobody seemed to be behaving to type; it was as though Carlton the Renaissance Man was being plagued by demons, by dark forces released to taunt and try him. And he would hold out – brazen, unflinching – before the assaults and machinations of lawyers and politicos and fake men of God, until one day – soon perhaps – he would emerge triumphant.

He gave a start. Above the hum of the air-conditioning there came a short ring at the door. He moved carefully, avoiding the windows, and squinted through the judas-eye. The image that greeted him was of a monstrous face as though reflected in a spoon – large mirror-glasses under a helmet with the vizor pushed up.

'Who is it?'

'Los Angeles Police. You Charles Carlton?'

'What's it in connection with, officer?'

'Just an inquiry, Mr Carlton. If you could let me in I'll explain.'

Warily, Carlton went through the ritual of opening the four locks, and finally released the chain and held the door open. 'Like Fort Knox, huh?'

'Yeah, but if a guy really wants to get in, he can get in. Believe me.'

Carlton caught a glimpse of a police motorcycle parked on its stand by the gate. The patrolman came in and began removing his helmet.

'Mind if I see your identification?'

'Sure.' The man wiped the sweat off his face and got out his PDLA badge.

'Mind telling me why you turn up now, when the heat's off?'

'What?' He had reddish hair and light reddish-brown eyes. 'Don't get you?'

'Well,' said Carlton, 'for the past ten days I've been

in hiding with my attorney, trying to escape the gentlemen of the Fourth Estate. The media.'

The patrolman nodded. 'Yeah I did hear something. Aren't you the one involved in the McIvor-kid case?'

'Yeah,' Carlton, with a weary shrug. 'You come to put the bracelets on me?'

'No. I come to make some inquiries.' He paused and licked his lips. 'Mind if I have a glass o' water?'

'Sure thing. Want something stronger?'

'Water's fine.'

Carlton went into the kitchenette and poured them two long glasses from the filter. 'Guaranteed as pure as the State of California.' He lifted his glass and watched the patrolman drink the whole glass in one. 'Jesus,' he gasped, 'I needed that. I was born up in the mountains. This city – whew!'

Carlton laughed. 'I'll drink to that.' He stopped and frowned. 'What brings you here, officer? You didn't just want a glass of water, did you?'

'No.' The patrolman put down his empty glass on the coffee-table. 'You know your neighbours well round here, Mr Carlton?'

Carlton shrugged. 'Some – but not well. You know how it is with us city folks, all locked up in our little white boxes . . .'

'Well we got in a report – Beverly Hills Precinct – saying a guy in a small car been seen hanging about here.'

'Where? When?'

'First report was late last night. Then the caller said he was out there again this morning.'

'Who?'

'That's what I kinda guessed you might know, Mr Carlton.'

'Look, officer, like I said I've been in hiding from the press. Last night was the first night I been here in ten days. So I haven't seen anything.'

The patrolman flipped open his notebook. 'First sighting 10.50 p.m. – dark Fiat saloon, registration 994233. Reported by B. Kessel. Know him?'

'Aw yeah. Retired film director. Enjoys making a big production out of everything and anything.'

'He reported seeing the car again at 4.30 a.m. today. And again at 9.30.'

'An insomniac.'

'Huh?'

'Doesn't matter. You call on him – you'll make his day. In the fifties he made some quite respectable crime movies. Anyway, what's this mystery-man supposed to look like?'

'We don't have a very detailed description. Male, white Caucasian, medium height, between forty and fifty, greying hair, sallow skin, wears dark glasses.'

'At four in the morning?'

'Well that's what the man said. He thought it didn't look right. And you know how it is in this neighbourhood – talk about Fort Knox, sometimes I think it's more like the Alamo!'

'What happened when you checked the number?'

'Rental company. Paid cash up front. Gave his name as Burroughs. Said he was a salesman from out of town. But someone or something must have tipped him off.

When we checked the rental office we found the car parked in a side street nearby, in a prohibited zone. And he didn't show up at the office – or at least, he ain't so far.'

'Maybe it's a lovers' tiff? Husband spying on his lady wife?'

'Yeah, sure. But it's those middle-aged guys take to sitting in the car all night – they're sometimes the ones that either blast their own brains out, or someone else's. I thank you for the water, Mr Carlton. And if you notice anything, call Beverly Hills and ask for Dwyer.'

'That you?'

'No, I'm Patrolman Degas. Dwyer's my boss. And he's a mean bastard. Good day, Mr Carlton.' And he walked back out into the muggy heat, adjusting his helmet as though it were some instrument of torture.

Chapter Twenty Four

The loud strains of a Heavenly Choir rolled out across the banks of seats, bouncing off the echo chambers of ten huge amplifiers close to the roof. The Temple of the Heavenly Word (proprietor, the Reverend Alan Weekes PhD), was the size and shape of a sports stadium, which is exactly what it had been before the original owners – the supervisors of the less than salubrious L.A. Precinct of Culver City – had gone bust and sold up to Evangelical Investments Inc., based in Bel Air, West Hollywood.

Several investigative journalists, from the East Coast as well as the West, had over the years tried to probe and unravel the devious finances and intricate power structure of the Heavenly Word, had either been frustrated or scared off by legal threats, and had ended no wiser than they'd begun. But the commonest conspiracy theories were that it was backed by the Mormons, the arms industry, a gay-lesbian cabal based in California, the Ku Klux Klan, the Libyans, and a syndicate of Wall Street junk-bond dealers. Separately or together, these were said to be trying to take over the country. But one thing was beyond dispute. The Heavenly Word was rich, and getting richer.

In the main make-up room – which had previously been part of the gym – the Rev. Alan Weekes reclined almost horizontally in a chair of deep red leather. His eyes were protected with sun-goggles against the over-head bars of ultraviolet, as were his two white-coated attendants – a young Vietnamese man who patted his smooth cheeks and massaged the slack muscles under his chin, while a Vietnamese girl practiced twau-koo on the soles of his feet. The Rev. Weekes was entirely naked, lying like a large white pig, sweating into the buttoned-down red leather hollows of the chair.

Twenty minutes later an alarm bell rang. Weekes was helped off the slimy wet chair and led the twenty yards to the sauna. Another twenty minutes later he emerged from the sauna and went through to the swimming pool. Weekes boasted that his day was divided into thirds – two thirds working, one third sleeping; and to give substance to this, he would cite some ancient mystic who described Man as incorporating three personalities – the Good, the Evil, and a Third Force that struggled for ascendancy between the other two. And the Rever-end Alan Weekes was that Third Force incarnate.

Apart from the obvious advantage of appealing to the restless hordes of Californians, ever hungry for new fads, new spiritual excitement – and quite unable to distinguish one from the other – it also offered Weekes a ready-made alibi against those who said he was a crook, a charlatan, a con-artist, a hustler, a phoney. For when attacked, he readily admitted his faults: these were the works of his Third Force taken over by his Bad Side, which must now be repelled, like a foreign invader . . . '*Bear with me, gentle brethren, and pray while I struggle in torment . . . !*'

One shrewd commentator had pointed out that this was the first modern evangelist to have turned evil – or the Bad Third – into a convertible moral currency, on an equal par with good. This presented his detractors, who were many, with a distinct disadvantage. For it is difficult to castigate a public figure for sins to which he readily admits.

But there was another reason – less vaunted – why criticism of Weekes and his movement was muted; he kept a team of lawyers on standby, used a newspaper cuttings service across the country, and taped every interview, every TV and radio programme in which he featured. Over the last ten years he had succeeded in winning over eight million dollars in libel suits – although he was usually always careful to settle out of court.

Weekes now emerged from the sauna, his pink flesh bearing an uncanny resemblance to fresh-cured ham, then plunged into the cold tub, before being helped back on to the leather chair, which the Vietnamese had thoroughly hosed down and dried.

The ultra-violet lamps had been switched off. In the

stillness a young man appeared behind his head, touching cool fingers to his temples. He had blown-dry hair and wore a white coat, like a young intern in a TV series. 'And how are we today, Cardinal!'

Weekes smiled beatifically. 'I am about to gird up my loins and draw the sword for battle, dear Henry.'

'On the TV – yeah, Reverend?'

'Where else, Henry – where else? One no longer finds the multitudes in the parks or at the street corners. One moves with the times, Henry . . .'

Henry went to work like a portrait painter, complete with pallet of make-up, powder, pencils and brushes. He whisked a thick sable brush over Weekes' brow, nose and chin; applying an array of subtly different make-up powder, to reduce shine, accentuate the voluptuous Bourbon profile, paint out the bags under his eyes, bury the folds under his chin.

Twenty minutes later – or nineteen, to be precise, since it had taken Weekes a minute to shower – the alarm sounded; the white-coated make-up artist stepped aside, and the two Vietnamese approached and began to dress him. A long white silk robe with huge sleeves; a shawl of deep purple silk round his shoulders; a little black folded cap, now fashionable among certain Muslim sects in America; bright red slippers, and in his hand a staff of malacca cane, with a knob of solid silver.

Weekes was admiring himself in the mirror, when his gold Rolex Oyster watch gave a sharp buzz, to warn him that it was almost time.

Alone, stepping carefully to avoid tripping over the folds of his robe – he had not yet entirely got used to

196

this particular attire – he emerged from the dark wings of the amphitheatre, walking towards a single shaft of blinding light from high above.

Music crashed around his ears – Brahms' First Symphony – while he knelt down in the tight circle of light, and made a curious gesture, lifting his hands, bowing his head, raising one clenched hand, then sweeping it down as though he were serving at tennis. (Connoisseurs of this kind of Californian witch-quackery observed that this ritual managed to combine something from the Catholic, the Islamic and Buddhist acts of obeisance, as well as providing a whiff of those other 20th-century religions, Fascism and Communism. At all events, the Rev. Weekes claimed to speak for all voices, 'however high, however low . . .').

A clapper-board sounded; a voice shouted, 'Action!' and the music swelled to a crescendo: Missa Solemnis, by Mozart.

Weekes stood up to his full height, raised his arms in their silk drapes, and stared into the blinding spotlight far above. In front of him the row upon row of seats were empty. Four camera crews, with sound and lighting technicians, were his only audience. Later, the films would be professionally edited, cut and pruned to maximum effect. For Weekes' oratory, in the raw, was often indigestible: a plethora of platitudes and homilies – half sermon, half rant.

He also had the reputation of speaking with a slight English accent, although it was not one that most Englishmen would recognise: a high, fluting intonation, at once unctuous and full of vague, oily menace.

'My friends! My dear, dear friends! My fellow citizens.' He paused; he smiled. The music had shrunk to a melodious march. The sound effects, including ecstatic applause, would be dubbed in later.

'We live, dear friends, in the *most beautiful State* in the *most beautiful country* on God's most beautiful Earth . . . !'

He attacked the smog, the rape of the Environment, the image-makers, 'sexploitation' of women, pornography, taxation, foreign aid – 'We give the taxes of our people to feed and clothe and arm half the countries of the world – and how do they repay us, these tiny rotting beggar-nations, each with its little flag at the U.N.? *How?* By burning down our embassies – blowing up our aircraft . . .

'Fellow citizens, we have lost our way. We send our wheat to Russia and guns to Africa. Yet to the four corners of the Earth *we are hated . . . !*'

Here he let out a long terrible wailing sound, like a well-bred wolf.

'. . . hated because we have become a new Babylon – here, in the City of Angels, we have become sick, debauched by wealth, blinded by science – led, oh God! by the morals of the TV set and the condom . . .'

He was into the last three minutes now. Again he paused, his expression bland, his big smooth face covered with a film of sweat.

'Poor, rich America . . . !' He raised his hands, then lowered them slowly across his chest.

'Forgive me – I talk politics. Better leave that to the politicians, just as it's better to leave the garbage to the garbage collectors!' He waited to allow time for the laughter to be inserted.

'Yet in the midst of all our wealth, all the treasures that the Earth has to give, we in this Babylon – this foul, sprawling, glittering slum – where it is as poisoned as the minds of the people who breathe it . . .

'Gentle brethren! Friends, Dear, dear friends. Today, living among us, are murderers!

'Friends, I speak not of the half-crazed junkies, the gang fights in our poorer areas . . .

'No, my friends. Those are the small potatoes – they get parcelled up and sent to the State Pen, or maybe the Chair.'

A deep hush in the auditorium. He raised his hand.

'No, I speak of murder most foul not under furtive darkness, but in the light of day . . . but hidden behind the mantle of respectability.

'Friends, I want you to close your eyes – while I try to tell you how it was . . .' He paused for only a moment, to wipe his eyes.

'Yes, my friends. I'll tell you how it was – for this particular killer, and for maybe two or three million other Americans who have killed like him. This guy I talk about – I cannot call him by name, because the law protects him, so I shall call him *this wanton killer* – had a good lunch downtown, then set off in his high-powered, brand-new sports car. He was feeling happy after his lunch, he was driving along a winding road near Holly-wood – he was driving fast and carefree . . . and then he crashes head-on into another car. His car is destroyed, but he escapes without a scratch. In the other car, they're not so lucky. A young mother and her five-year-old child are crushed to death.'

He stood with both arms outstretched, and repeated slowly, 'A young mother, oh gentle friends – a young mother and her child – *crushed to death*!' He hurled these words in a dreadful half-scream that had the ring of a mad King Lear.

This time he stopped, brushed his hands across his eyes, swallowed hard, and said, in a voice cracked with emotion, 'Please bear with me, gentle Americans . . . !'

The production manager had begun to make the winding up signal: forty seconds to go.

'That young killer, I must tell, will *not* spend the rest of his natural life in a cell. Oh no! He'll go out and hire a sharp lawyer, and he'll probably get off with a fine and a six-month suspension of his licence.'

'That man killed two people. Destroyed a whole family. And he's out there somewhere, probably watching this programme.'

'*Hi, fella! How d'you feel?*'

The production manager, a rubbery young man in a T-shirt with the legend, *I HELP GOD AND HE HELPS ME*, came springing up. 'Great stuff, Cardinal! It's one of the best – even stronger, I think, than the one on AIDS.'

'Thank you, Saul. I wasn't quite so sure about the politics – aid to the Third World is a long way from our killers on the road.'

'Ah no, they'll love it. A bit o' variety, it's good

200

showbiz. And when we get the sound-effects – the applause, it'll slay 'em out there!'

'What are we using for applause?' Weekes had lowered his voice, reluctant to mention this subterfuge in more than a whisper.

'Hollywood Bowl 1987, mixed with Red Sox versus New York Yankies 1988.'

Weekes always checked and double-checked this detail, ever since the time he'd given one of these 'Gospel Hot-Shots' on a Sunday evening and, in the first break for applause, several women could be clearly heard screaming for Liberace. It had rather spoilt Weekes' evening.

'When will you have the rushes?' he asked.

'Tomorrow at ten suit you?'

'That's fine. I'd like Roz Acker and her people to get a look at it before it goes out. It ties in with her theme of getting drunk-drivers treated like common criminals. Only *discretion*, Saul. I don't want anyone else to know. Okay?'

'Okay, Cardinal. Message received and understood.' And he smiled, as he watched the big white-robed figure padding back to the leather couch to have his make-up removed; and as he watched, he thought, What a jerk! What a big fat phoney loada pig-shit! Someday someone's going to bust his ass wide open! *Splat!* Hell, it might even be me . . .

Chapter Twenty Five

As the hot muggy day dragged on, Carlton found himself growing uncommonly nervous. Certainly the agony of the morning – given one hour to clear his desk, without warning – would normally have been eased by an afternoon's stiff drinking in the Rackets Club. But he'd given up drinking. He was going to tough it out, just like he was going to tough out his problems, eyeball-to-eyeball, and do battle with whoever and whatever came to hand.

He did go to the Rackets Club, but only for a light lunch and a swim. Some of the other members, he noticed, glanced at him and muttered to each other; but none came near him. As it was in working hours, most of these members were old, with too much time on their hands: just the sort who sat in front of the TV and saw everything.

The hell with them. He had his own life to lead. But now, as six o'clock came nearer, he began to plan his strategy, probe those areas where Janice was most vulnerable, and reinforce those where he was. He didn't know why he always thought of love – or at least the progress of an erotic quest – in terms of military history. Certainly, once you stripped away the emotional overkill – the obsession of falling in love, which the Ancient Greeks considered a form of madness – what you were left with was a game between two people, each trying to outwit and outflank the other. In normal times it was a thoroughly enjoyable game, with a luscious prize at the end.

But today Carlton realised he was sick with apprehension. He had only to think of Janice, and he felt that empty sinking feeling; and when he thought of her body, of how it was between the sheets, in the shower, in the sea, he felt the sickening dread of losing her. Since the accident they had hardly spoken to each other. Shock, they'd said. Give her time to get over it. So she'd gone to Bear Lake, and now she was back and he was about to face her.

He went through the meeting in his mind, like sketching out some scene for a TV commercial . . . She would have to be wooed, her jangled nerves soothed. He would ask her to dinner, and show that he was no longer drinking; and he would not try to take her to bed, unless she made it quite clear that she wanted to.

But that left one problem. Her performance yesterday in court. How was he to tackle it? Unless perhaps she tackled it first. Was she really unable to remember what had happened that afternoon? Had she really *meant* what she said – or was it all just a side-effect from shock?

He'd have to clear this up. Or could it just be ignored? It couldn't be, of course, because *next week she was going to have to go through the whole ghastly ritual all over again*. And he knew – as she must know – that if she repeated her performance of yesterday, that would be the end. He would lose her, on top of whatever the court might decide to take too.

He paused by a mirror in the hall and stood for a moment contemplating what Californians like to call 'a combative role-model'. What, he wondered, would General Patten have done in a situation like this?

As the evening approached, he concentrated – as Patten would have done – on logistics. And here he was again reminded of the nuisance of being without a car in L.A. He'd have to call a cab, from either Santa Monica or Bel Air. Both lines were busy. It was coming up to the Friday rush-hour, of course.

Finally, he got through to Bel Air and was told there was a forty minute delay, minimum. He knew there was some sort of bus, but God alone knew when it left. Or he could walk, which would take the best part of ninety minutes – if he wasn't picked up or shot at as a vagrant. Nobody walks in L.A.

Finally, with the clock past five, he called the Bel Air Hotel and asked for their *de luxe* chauffeur-driven limo service. Two hundred bucks an hour, minimum rental time three hours, and double for after seven o'clock.

He made that a grand total of eight hundred dollars.

Was this a sensible way to go about rewooing his long-time partner? Patten would have made a tactical withdrawal. Okay, so Carlton was going to engage the enemy head-on. Anyway, hiring a limo was no crazier than anything else that had happened to him in the past ten days.

He finished dressing and smoked three cigarettes while he waited. It was half-past five, and still no sign of the limo. He went outside and saw a car across the street with two men in it. As he appeared, one of them got out and produced a dark object from under his coat. In a flash Carlton remembered the patrolman – the warning about the night-prowler . . . Christ, he's got a gun! – and he ducked down and tripped over his foot, as he scrambled back inside. Only then did he realise it had been a camera pointing at him . . .

So they were back, the slimeballs! He was a prisoner in his own home. He felt hot with anger, and thought of charging out again and confronting them, dragging them both out of the car, smashing the camera . . . And spending the next two or three hours in the Beverly Hills Precinct station, with a couple of friendly journos who'd spread the mess all across tomorrow's papers.

He willed himself to keep away from the window, to wait patiently for a limo that was going to cost him eight hundred bucks.

It was a quarter to six. The bell sounded. He sprang up and opened it. It was still bright enough not to need a flash. The one behind took his picture, while the one in front smiled and said, 'Mr Carlton, we heard a

205

rumour you were fired from your ad. agency. True?'

'Go to hell.'

'Thank you, Mr Carlton . . .' As he slammed the door shut.

They were back in the car, watching, when the limo drew up. It was a midnight-blue Fleetwood sedan. The chauffeur got out and came towards the house. He was a good-looking black in a pale blue uniform, with white gloves, flared trousers and highly polished knee-boots. Across the road, the newsman with the camera took his time, shooting Carlton with a zoom-lens as the chauffeur held the door open for him.

'We're very late,' Carlton said, as the car started.

'I am sorry, sir. Wilshire and Sunset are both blocked. Traffic's backed up right down to the Ocean.'

'Know a quick way to the Bel Air Clinic, Pasadena?'

'Yes, sir, they gave me the address. If you'll bear with me, I'll try some of the back ways.'

'Okay, do it.'

'You want to watch TV, Sir?'

'Why not?' he said. At ten bucks a minute, it might almost pay to take out a thirty-second spot – *Brave young executive, persecuted by the media, victimised by ruthless politicians and self-seeking evangelists . . . Seeks gainful employment. Anything legal.*

The TV was set in maplewood, next to the cocktail cabinet. Carlton sat back and watched the ads coming up before the six o'clock news. He looked out and tried to see where they were. The chauffeur was avoiding the freeways and driving down quiet wooded streets, lazy in the hot evening gloom.

He watched the News and was only mildly relieved that it didn't have anything about a bright young adman taking a poke at his attorney and then getting the sack . . . Then the weather. No ocean breezes. Smog likely in all areas. More ads.

Less than ten minutes to go, and they hadn't even crossed the Pasadena Freeway. Heavy music filled the quiet of the car. A big moon-faced man in a white robe, like a Klansman, began a curious ritual, bowing, saluting – and he thought, Oh no, a God slot! He heard the man cry out, '*Friends! Dear friends! Fellow-citizens . . . !*' – and silenced him with the remote-control; and instead, caught a Rock concert – the Stones at the Hollywood Bowl – on FM radio.

But this did not compensate for the four lanes of creeping traffic along the Pasadena Freeway, which the chauffeur could not bypass. 'Mighty sorry, Sir. It's always the same – Fridays – the Freeway's jammed.'

Carlton wondered if Janice would see it that way. One of her characteristics was extremely punctuality, which she expected others to share. Some of their worst rows had been about his being late. Excuses, excuses – he'd tried them all.

He took a deep breath, taking advantage of the air-conditioning. The Stones were in fine voice. He sat with eyes closed, knowing there was nothing he could do now. Just wait. He dozed off, with the beat hammering the adrenalin through his brain.

He woke suddenly. It was 6.42. The limo had stopped almost opposite the Clinic at the Brasserie. The black chauffeur holding the door open. Carlton looked for a sight of Janice in the glass-fronted porch. He didn't particularly want her to see the limo – even less when she discovered he'd been fired . . . She could be funny about that sort of thing. Prudent housekeeping, they called it.

He'd already charged the $800 to his Amex Gold Card. The chauffeur was still holding the door open, and Carlton put a fifty-dollar bill in his white cotton hand. 'Thanks.'

'Thank *you*, Sir! And have a nice evening!'

Carlton hurried into the Brasserie. The Happy Hour was well underway, and the place was packed. He struggled through a tiny jungle of potted plants, and came out at the bar, with the long dining room beyond.

He stood for several minutes, chin down, head bowed, his eyes flitting across the tables, down the bar, towards the cloakrooms, and back to the bar. There was no sign of Janice. This surprised him less, perhaps, than his own behaviour. For perhaps the first time in his life – certainly his life in L.A. – he was actively seeking anonymity, dreading eye-contact with someone he knew . . .

In short, he was behaving like a pariah. And if you behave like a pariah, sooner or later you become one.

The barman, a hunky Hispanic with flat wet hair and gaucho side-burns, asked him what he wanted to drink. He said, 'I'm looking for a girl – I'm late and we were due to meet at 6.15. I wondered if she might have left a message. Name of Rhodes – Dr Rhodes.'

The barman frowned. 'You Dr Rhodes?'

'No, no, no! The girl – *she's* Dr Rhodes. Very pretty,

honey-blonde hair – very striking. Terrific figure. Quite tall, but not too tall . . .'

The Hispanic gave a brilliant smile: 'I'd sure like to be sick with a doctor like that around!'

'Think I'm kidding?'

'Me, Sir? I'm just paid to serve drinks. Whattya want?'

Carlton ordered a fresh orange juice and Perrier. It was nearly seven o'clock. He stood with his back to the bar and watched the doors, wondering if this could be the most expensive stand-up in American history?

Chapter Twenty Six

Kuzak switched off the video recorder and ejected the tape. 'I'd like to take that big fat creep and string him up by his balls and then see what came out.'

'So violent!' Ann Kelsey said, with heavy irony. 'What can be the matter?'

'I just don't like seeing a client – even an ex-client – being stitched up. I don't like injustice. In fact, I'm allergic to it.'

While he was speaking, Abby Perkins looked in. 'Another carton of yoghurt's arrived, Ann – courtesy of Mr Petersen, of course.'

'You're joking?' said Ann.

'I am not.' Abby laughed. 'Why don't we settle the case by you agreeing, Ann, never to eat yoghurt for the rest of your natural life?'

'Wouldn't work. Ann's already hooked on the stuff,'

said Kuzak. 'Back there in her office it's turning into a health farm. Cigarettes are out, coffee's on the way out, and tea's making a last heroic stand. Poor Stuart's wasting away, like one of those posters for famine relief.'

'What are you so worried about anyway, Ann?' said Kuzak. 'You've got the figure of a young girl!'

'Oh my! Oh my! Michael, what has come over you? What do I tell Stuart?'

'Don't tell him anything. How is that damn-fool case with the slug in the yoghurt coming along, anyway?'

'Nix. We interviewed all the employees at Dairyland – we've taken affidavits from them all – and we've photographed all the mechanical processes, from pure milk to the sealed carton.'

'So?'

'The plaintiff still insists he found a slug in his yoghurt.'

'Can he prove it?'

'Probably not. But that's not really the point. If the case goes to court – and even if we win – the publicity will ruin Dairyland.'

Kuzak nodded, frowning. 'Know what I'd do? I'd run a trace on this guy. If it's a scam, I give odds-on he's tried it before. Threaten litigation, settle out of court, then vamoose! Over the State line, lie low for a bit, then do it again.'

'I've got an even better idea!' Abby cried. 'Why doesn't Michael take over the yoghurt, and Ann and Stuart can look after Carlton. Stuart's a sucker for punishment – and anyway judges *and* juries like him. A rarity these days.'

They both looked at Kuzak. 'Who said I was off the Carlton case?' he growled.

This time they both looked at Abby. Ann Kelsey had been the only independent witness to the fight between Kuzak and Carlton, albeit in self-defence, and they were both determined to keep it that way. For a successful attorney to hit his client is a sure way to finish up selling matches on Skid Row.

Abby smiled, with feline innocence. 'Well, you know, getting cited for contempt . . .'

'Judge Sachs is a copper-bottomed sonofabitch!' said Kuzak.

'Exactly. That's why I feel mighty sorry for that guy, Carlton. I mean, he looks like a big, beefy dreamboat, but I wouldn't be surprised if he wasn't all soft and gooey inside, like an overgrown schoolboy.'

Ann Kelsey laughed. 'Sounds as though you're hooked, Abby! But where did you meet him? Not here in the office?'

'I saw him on TV.' – and as she spoke, her neat pretty features flushed pink, and she lowered her eyes.

Ann Kelsey said, 'I think I smell something here. Abby – you didn't *just* see him on the TV, did you?'

'Well – as a matter of fact – well . . .'

'Come on, Abby, spit it out!' said Ann Kelsey.

Kuzak was watching, listening closely. He wondered if this might turn out to be one of those cases where there's a clash of interests – if not worse.

Abby said, 'You remember my husband – correction, my ex-husband?'

'Not intimately,' said Ann Kelsey.

'Well –' Abby's brow puckered, as though she were set on a course that she already regretted. '– Well, when I was still married we sometimes went to Malibu at weekends and there were house parties on the beach. All-night affairs, sometimes . . .'

'Jesus!' said Kuzak. 'This is getting interesting.'

'You can't leave us now, Abby,' said Ann Kelsey.

Abby was blushing and stammering, now thoroughly confused. 'Well, if you haven't already guessed, I met Chuck Carlton at one of these parties.'

'Did you?' Kuzak said.

'Did I what?'

'C'mon, Abby! Like babies are brought by the storks.'

She collected herself and took a deep breath. 'Actually, no. I didn't. *We* didn't. You may not believe me, but I was faithful to my husband. It may sound crazy now, but I was.'

'So where does Carlton fit in?' said Kuzak.

'Well, when we met – at this beach party – I remember thinking he was one of the best-looking men I'd ever seen. I guess I showed it, because my husband started getting nasty. He was drunk, of course, and he started making nasty suggestions about me and Chuck Carlton. Chuck had had a good deal to drink as well, and he threw a punch at my husband and broke his nose. He tried to date me a couple of times, but I

213

decided to be a good girl, in spite of everything. And a lot of damn good it's done me!'

'That's all?' said Kuzak. 'No kissing, no fumbling?'

'You have a dirty mind, Michael. The point is, I actually quite *liked* Carlton . . .'

'He sounds just divine,' said Ann Kelsey sceptically.

'It may sound odd,' Abby went on. 'But I liked him *in spite of* his good looks. There was something very eager and yet – vulnerable . . . You know?'

'Sure we know,' said Kuzak. 'It's called cradle snatching.'

But Abby Perkins was set on a course, and she was not going to stop now. 'The few times I met him, I used to just think – well, at that party, anyway – how it would be nice to look after him . . .' She hesitated. 'I feel the same now – even more so, perhaps. Just seeing him on TV, and the way they're all treating him.'

'Well, Abby, he sure needs someone to look after him *now*,' said Kuzak. 'In spades!'

'You've let him go, I suppose?'

'Why d'you say that?' Kuzak asked suspiciously. He'd been so darned careful not to let the full story out. He owed that as much to himself as to Carlton.

'I just heard you were having problems,' Abby said. 'Someone in the D.A.'s office told me, off the record, that Judge Sachs was right out of line . . . that if it came to court, Carlton would have good grounds to appeal, claiming *a priori* prejudice in the Inquiry.'

'And who was this little bird that twittered to you, honey?' Kuzak was thoroughly interested now.

'No, Mike, it was off the record. So *nix*. Okay?'

'Okay.' Kuzak nodded grimly, wondering where this was getting them, if anywhere at all.

There was a tap at the door and Douglas Brackman's gloomy visage stared in at them. 'Anyone doing any work round here? Or are you just catching up on *Sesame Street*?'

Kuzak came to attention and saluted. 'All present and correct!'

Brackman came closer. 'This is important, Michael. In my office . . .'

Kuzak frowned. 'I was planning on going home in half an hour – catch the serial on Channel 5.'

'In my office, Mike. The law waits for no man.'

'So?' – Kuzak followed him out into the corridor – 'What gives?'

'It's Carlton.'

'What's he done now? Taken a dive off the top of the City Hall?'

'Not quite.' Brackman led the way into his office and closed the door behind them both. 'Mike, when did you last see Carlton?'

Kuzak knew he'd be more than a fool if he lied to Brackman. 'Yesterday evening – just about this time. We had a row. He stormed out. Then, when I heard he'd got fired, I went to his house late this afternoon. There were a couple of newspapermen waiting in a car, and they said Carlton had just gone out. In a chauffeur-driven limo, for Chrissake.'

'You didn't hang around at all?'

'No – why should I? He'd hardly go out with a chauffeur to get the groceries? Anyway, what is all this?'

215

'Did you see any police round there?'

'No. Just the newsmen. Douglas, what *is* this . . . ?'

'He's in trouble, Mike. Somebody's out to kill him.'

Chapter Twenty Seven

Carlton was hunched over the bar, hemmed in by two noisy couples who were making love to each other at the tops of their voices, while Carlton sucked on a cigarette and wondered what in hell to do next. He held out his orange juice for a refill, when he felt a touch on his arm.

He turned. Janice was standing right behind him. She was wearing an oatmeal linen suit with a loose white belt and a wide-brimmed white hat. Her eyes were shaded by the brim, and her face was unfashionably pale, in a city where suntans come out of bottles.

But Dr Janice Rhodes was of an altogether higher order. She knew this, and Carlton, in his carefree loving way, knew it too. He kissed her on the mouth, then drew back from the bar to give her room. 'I thought I'd missed you, honey. What can I get you?'

'I'll just have a coffee. I was held up – there was a crisis, a kid with major concussion – fell off a swing.'

He realised it was going to be impossible to have a conversation here – which was no doubt why the Brasserie was so popular. Was it also why she'd chosen it? He got the coffee and another orange juice, then guided her over to where there was a free table under a baby palm.

'It's wonderful to see you, honey! You make me feel alive again.' He beamed at her, a bright eager smiling face like a boy about to open his Christmas presents. 'Have you been okay?'

She gave him a long level stare, neither reproachful nor accusatory, but just a little wistful, a little sad. He waited, still smiling, and put his hand on hers, anticipating what she would have to say about her evidence in court.

But she said nothing about the court. She removed her hand, not pointedly, but in order to drink her coffee. She drank half the cup, patted the napkin to her lips, and said, 'Chuck. I've come to say goodbye to you.'

The smile froze on his mouth, and the roar of the Brasserie was suddenly silenced, replaced by a mighty ringing in his ears. If he'd wanted to say anything, he wouldn't have been able to. He watched her mouth, her eyes, trying to keep her in focus, to hang on to anything of hers that might anchor him to reality.

'I've given my notice at the clinic – till the end of the month – and I've booked a trip to Europe. To England.

I've got a job as a temporary *locum* – that's what they're called there – at a little hospital in a place called Cirencester. I'll be there for four months, then I'm going to Germany to look around, and I thought I might try working in Hungary. They're very advanced there – the Peto Institute . . .'

Chuck's arms and legs had gone all wobbly. The breath was coming through his mouth in a tight creaking sound, and he realised that he'd turned a very odd colour. She broke off and said, 'Chuck, are you feeling all right?'

'I'm just fine,' he said. 'I lost my job today, I may have to face a criminal charge – maybe jail – and now . . .'

She said, 'Please don't get upset, Chuck. Please.'

'What am I supposed to do? Dance on the table?'

'I just want you to be mature about it. We're adults . . .'

Carlton slammed his hand on the table. 'Oh mature shit, Janice! Save that for the child psychologists and the welfare people! For Chrissake, what's *happened* between us? Is there another guy? Okay, tell me. Is he going with you to Europe? Don't I have a right to know?'

'Of course you do. I am going to Europe alone. There isn't anybody else. I am just going away for a few months and I am not going to see you again.' She spoke with a quiet chilling determination. He knew, before he even opened his mouth, that he was licked.

He said, in a hoarse croak, 'Why? What – *what happened*?'

'I was going to leave the clinic, anyway. I got offered the place in England nearly a month ago . . .'

'But that was before the accident! I don't understand . . . Why didn't you tell me? Why *couldn't* you tell me?'

'Because I didn't think you'd want to know.'

'Aw c'mon Janice. You're not being honest. Or should I say, *mature*?'

She gave him another long passionless stare. 'All right, Chuck. I'll tell you. But on one condition.'

'Yeah?'

'I don't want any recriminations, and I don't want you trying to get me back – not in L.A., not in England, not any place. I'm going away alone and I'm going to start all over again.'

He just stared back at her, his knuckles white round his empty glass of orange juice. She went on:

'About five weeks ago I missed my period. The old story, huh? I had the test and it was positive. I thought of telling you, but I knew – I just *knew* – that you'd be about as pleased as if I'd jumped up and down on your head.'

'Oh for Chrissake, Janice . . . !' He looked at her in utter misery. 'Is that why you shafted me in court yesterday?'

'I was coming to that. Two days before the crash I made an appointment to have an abortion. I half hoped the shock of the accident would have done it for me. It didn't. So I had it done here in L.A. and went up to Bear Lake to rest. And to think. Maybe I thought a lot of crazy things, but I was convinced that the dead foetus and that dead child were somehow linked up. I still do.

I feel you and I, Chuck, have come under what some cultures call "the Evil Eye".'

'Aw Janice baby, for Christ's sake, this is California – not Africa or the Middle East!'

She shrugged. 'Maybe it's crazy. But it's what I feel. I feel it deep, deep inside, and there's nothing you can say or do that'll make the slightest difference.'

'You think I killed your baby, like I killed that child?'

'Not deliberately. But if it hadn't been for you, they'd both be alive now.'

For a moment Carlton thought there'd been an earthquake: the whole floor tilted and he felt a giddy screaming noise in his ears, as he grabbed desperately on to the table. Several other people saw what was happening and thought he was drunk. Carlton, in a futile effort to impress her, said, 'I'm not drunk, Janice. *I am not drunk!*'

Somebody had grabbed his arm, steady but firm – 'take it easy, soldier . . . left, right . . . steady as she goes . . . !' – and Carlton's face was parting the palm fronds, as he was helped into the toilet, bending over the basin, his head plunged under the icy tape. 'Okay, soldier?'

He was a big pleasant-looking all-American boy – the kind that liberated Iwo Jima and didn't jibe at paying taxes to rebuild Europe.

Carlton straightened up, blinked at himself in the mirror, then gave his saviour a hangdog grin. 'That's what you get drinking orange juice – *honest!*'

'You want me call a doctor?'

'I'll be okay. My girl just threw me over.'

'Girls are like buses. There'll be another one along, don't worry.'

Carlton thanked him, steadied himself, then marched back into the bar-restaurant. He knew what he would find before he got there – he was so certain that it was not even a shock when he reached the table to find strangers sitting in their places – a fat young man with a crew-cut and a raunchy looking girl in denim hot-pants.

A waiter touched his sleeve. 'The lady said she had to leave. Okay?' The man's voice had a slight cutting edge, as if to say, *You wanna get asshole pissed, buddy, you go somewhere else* . . .

'Can you get me a cab?'

'Sure.' The waiter went over to a phone by the door. Carlton gave him his address and waited.

'Did you see the girl leave?'

'Yeah. 'Bout five minutes ago.'

'Did you get her a cab?'

'Nope. Guess she had her own transport.'

'Sure. Thanks.' Carlton walked out into the muggy Californian dusk and waited for the cab.

Chapter Twenty Eight

'Death-threats in this business are a dime a dozen,' said Kuzak. 'If the cops had to provide a watch on every Joe in this city who thought he was at risk, they'd need a damned army!'

'There are threats and threats,' said Brackman. 'The reason I think this one might be more serious is something I learnt half an hour ago. Something that's going to make big news tomorrow morning. And is going to run and run.'

'I'm listening, Douglas.'

'Grace called me from the D.A.'s office. She particularly asked that you be told. Apparently, six months ago the IRS started investigations into the Hot-Gospeller, Alan Weekes, and discovered as much as a hundred million dollars in tax evasion. Anyway, as his outfit started to unravel, all kinds of things came to light. To put it simply, the F.B.I. and the Justice Department got involved, and a lot of people's telephones got tapped – among others, that of Judge Roz Acker.

'The Revenue boys were happy just with Weekes, but it seems the Justice Department have got very, very sore at both Weekes and Acker, and what they describe as a gross degradation of justice, corruption of the due legal system, infringements of human rights, and abuse of at least three Amendments of the Constitution. And the Joe Doe whose case gets the most attention is that of your boy, Chuck Carlton.'

Douglas Brackman gave one of his rare, dark smiles. 'It seems that those two tapes – of Acker and Weekes – are going to be made prime exhibits in whatever case finally comes to court. Most important, Grace says the D.A. himself is due to put out a statement to the effect that any further proceedings against Carlton would be a perversion of justice.'

'That's terrific!' Kuzak said. 'At least the D.A. realises he wouldn't get a fair trial.'

Brackman continued, 'What's more, according to Grace, he's going to state that in American law a man cannot be tried twice for the same crime. *And Carlton has already been tried on television* – particularly the paid air-time by Weekes and Acker, plus the organised picketing of the courts, in what could lead to criminal charges of conspiracy to pervert the course of justice. In short, your boy is vindicated – and this time tomorrow he'll be on the way to being a national hero!'

Kuzak leapt up and punched the air. 'The American

Dream – the Lone Ranger triumphs against the forces of darkness. I like it!'

'Well –' Brackman shook his head, 'The Justice Department don't come out of it too badly.'

Kuzak paused, then nodded. 'But the death threat . . . ?'

'Sure,' Brackman said. 'As long as your boy, Carlton, is being railroaded into the State Pen by certain parties already mentioned, a certain other party would probably let the People versus Carlton do their worst. But when it gets to see the headlines tomorrow – with TV bytes from the Attorney-General in Washington, naming Carlton as a *victim* – then that individual is going to get mighty sore . . . He's going to feel cheated.'

'Maybe he already feels cheated?' Kuzak was standing up, starting towards the door. 'You say this isn't going to break till tomorrow?'

'Well, according to Grace . . .'

'Look, if Grace van Owen knows, at least a dozen other people know, and newspapers and TV don't take that much notice of embargoed stories – not *big* stories like this.'

'Where are you going?'

'I'm going to warn Carlton – what d'you think?'

'Be careful, Michael.'

Kuzak grinned. 'If you wanted me to be careful, you should have kept all this to yourself!'

225

Chapter Twenty Nine

Carlton sat sprawled in the back of the cab, vaguely conscious of the motion of his body in relation to the earth below him: the swaying, the undulating, slowing, accelerating . . . He had the curious sensation of being anaesthetised, as though pain, misery, danger were no longer of any account.

He knew he should be worrying about Janice. He should be trying to find her, to reason with her, to talk her out of this crazy plan to get to England and – where was it? – Hungary . . . He didn't think about the baby – the abortion – just as he had spent nearly two weeks refusing, quite successfully, to think about that child in the crash.

He knew that his reactions were not quite normal. That passing out in the Brasserie was not the normal reaction of a grown man because his girl's just chucked him.

The driver looked at him in the mirror and said, 'We're on Sepulveda – what number was it?'

It was just two blocks on. He told the driver to put him down here. He needed the walk. In the time that it had taken to get here from the Brasserie, the light had faded and it was now a warm velvet night, suddenly rich with exotic scents – one of those nights that almost persuade Californians to forget the awful man-made squalor all around them.

Carlton was walking rather slowly, like an invalid taking his first steps after a long illness. The street was very quiet. From a long way away he could hear the muffled drone of the Freeway. There were cars parked on both sides, and he noticed that the two newsmen in the car had gone. He didn't care anyway. He didn't care about anything very much now. He would let himself in and have a shower, then take the last two of Janice's sleeping-pills, and crash out and to hell with all of them . . .

He opened the door, turned on the lights, went through the hall. The light was winking again on his answering machine. He left it, beginning to loosen his collar, undo his trousers, moving towards the shower and jacuzzi, and remembered that he hadn't eaten anything. That was perhaps why he'd passed out in the Brasserie. In fact, he hadn't been eating too well since the accident.

He turned on the jacuzzi, watching the clear water swirling round like wheels within wheels. He stepped

227

out of his clothes, and at that moment a tiny bell triggered by instinct began to sound in his head. What was
it? He hadn't seen or heard anything. Then he knew:
it was a smell. Very faint, and unfamiliar. A dry musky
smell, not unpleasant, but unfamiliar. Not a woman's
scent, he thought, as he lowered himself on to the
middle step of the jacuzzi – and then he knew, with
sudden insight, that it was a smell of aftershave . . .

If his instinct for survival had been as acute as it
should have been, he would have panicked, and probably died as a result. As it was, he was already like a
man sleep-walking, inured to the slings and arrows of
outrageous fortune, and by now almost bored by the
drudgery of facing another day.

The man made no sound, above the rustling of the
water jets, as he came up to Carlton, standing just
behind him on the green glazed tiles. Carlton twisted
his head and looked up at him. He hardly recognised
him. He was wearing brown slacks, yellow socks and
black moccasins. His face was a vague greyish blur
against the overhead lighting. He was holding with both
hands a double-barrelled shotgun, and his finger was
crooked round both triggers.

He said, 'You wanna know how I got in?'

'I know – you got in through the keyhole, like Peter
Pan.'

'Who's he?'

Carlton laughed. He actually found it funny. And the
laughter completely confused the gunman.

'You crazy, or summin? You crazy fucker – I'm
gonna teach yer, gonna make yer crawl like an animal!

228

You know – you know – *you know what you done,
don't yer?*'

'You're in my house,' Carlton said, in almost a drawl,
'so be kind enough to watch your manners.'

'*What!* You know who I am?' There was a coarse
hysteria in the voice – a voice warped by hatred and
imagined wrongs. 'You killed my wife! You killed my
boy – my five-year-old boy!' – he was leaning down
slightly, speaking in little more than a whisper – 'my
whole family – *you killed them . . .* !'

In a funny detached way Carlton knew what the next
line would be. It couldn't be anything else. The man
was going to say, '*And now I'm going to kill you!*' He
couldn't say anything else. And Carlton had approximately two seconds to take the man.

Without moving his back, he grabbed the man's legs
with his naked arm and yanked both feet towards him.
The man lost his balance, struggled wildly, waving his
arms, trying to get a hold of Carlton's wet slippery
body, while at the same time keeping hold of the gun.
Carlton saw one moccasin plunge into the water, and
then he roused himself – drawing on all his reserves of
strength, of suppressed rage and anguish since that
night when he'd first seen this man in Emergency at the
Washington Hospital; and he went for the man in the
quickest, nastiest way he knew, by stabbing at his gen-
itals with stiffened fingers, twice, as hard as he could.
The man screamed, still thrashing in the water like a
great fish, his clothes clinging to him, dark and shiny,
his face contorted – and then the explosion. Or rather,
two explosions, overlapping, and Carlton felt a huge

229

thump against his shoulder, and a slightly lesser, sharper pain in his side.

He got hold of the gun, the barrel hot under his wet hand, and he felt it loosen from the man's grip. Carlton swung it round, in a long lazy arc, and brought it down with a crack on the side of the man's head. The sound was barely audible above the roaring aftermath of the twin explosions.

The water in the jacuzzi was rapidly turning from pink to dark red. Carlton looked down and saw half his body emptying blood into swirling whirlpools. The pain was only just beginning. The gun, he saw, was under the water. So was Colin McIvor.

Carlton still had the strength to reach down and dragged the waterlogged body to the side, then up the steps, laying it out on the tiles. There was blood everywhere now. And a terrible noise – insistent, hammering, pitiless . . .

McIvor was barely conscious, bleeding from the head, his face like wax. Carlton started to rise, then doubled up and was violently sick into the jacuzzi. Most of it was orange-juice from the Brasserie, which blended spectacularly with the blood.

From somewhere behind him there was a tremendous *crash*! and three men came lumbering through the broken front door. Two of them were policemen, with guns drawn; the other was Michael Kuzak.

'Jesus Christ! *Holy Mother!*' one of the policemen said.

Carlton peered at Kuzak, and frowned. 'Mike, Janice threw me over, and now I got shot . . . !'

'You're gonna be all right!' Kuzak said, and turned to the two policemen, pointing down at Colin McIvor. 'That's the one . . .'

But at this point, Carlton lost consciousness.

*

Carlton had lost almost 2 pints of blood, and was reckoned to have been lucky to pull through. They'd had to operate on his leg, but they saved it, although he was told he'd always walk with a slight limp and he'd have to forget about skiing.

Kuzak was sitting beside the bed, looking rather pleased with himself. He had arrived at the house seconds before the double explosion, and just as a patrol car came past. The local Precinct had had their eye on McIvor for two days now; but this didn't prevent Kuzak from allowing the press and TV to compare him to the Cavalry riding to the rescue in the last reel.

With him by the bed was a petite, very pretty girl whom Carlton found vaguely, distantly familiar. 'Santa Monica – three summers ago?'

He gave her a glazed grin. He was still on a drip-feed and his lips felt hideously chapped. 'You're married to what's his name – and I kissed you . . .'

'You sure did! You kissed me, I divorced my husband, and now I'm just plain Abby Perkins –'

'You with Mike here?' Carlton asked, mildly interested.

231

Kuzak answered, 'Abby's one of the bright young stars of McKenzie Brackman. In fact, she's just won a case for us without ever going to court . . .'

'Mike, it wasn't just me.'

Kuzak had turned to Carlton. 'She was brilliant, Chuck. We had this case – I may have told you – of a guy trying to sue Dairyland because he claimed to have found a slug in a tub of yoghurt. We did all the background research, but it was one of those cases where, while the guy couldn't exactly prove his case, we couldn't exactly *disprove* it . . . *Ergo*, there were compelling grounds for our client to settle out of court. Then Abby ran a few traces – she was originally brought in to assist Ann Kelsey with the spadework. She called the P.D.'s in a number of States, and also ran a check through the national newspaper archives. And *hey presto*! – in the last eight years there have been two identical cases – one in Florida, one in Arizona. Different names, but – with a bit of checking – Abby finds it's the same guy.' Kuzak smiled at her.

'Actually, it was the guy himself who gave me the most help,' she said. 'You see, the scam in Florida attracted a lot of media attention. The guy was threatening to sue a fruit company in Tampa for selling him a can of sliced grapefruit which contained – wait for it! – parts of a chopped up cotton-mouth moccasin – one of the most dangerous snakes in the world.'

Carlton pulled a face of genuine disgust. 'How did he get caught?'

'Oh he blabbed in a bar – that sort of thing. Did three years in the slammer, then tried it again in Arizona –

a bit less sensational this time – a couple of earthworms in a can of Calypso beans. They caught him that time because he tried to forge a cheque. Dumb.'

Carlton nodded. 'I hope your client is duly grateful?'

'Oh he is, believe me!' Kuzak groaned. 'He's spent the past two weeks bombarding us with samples of his yoghurt, and yesterday Ann and Abby each got two great bouquets of roses – one red, one white. Their offices look like a call girl's bedroom!'

She stood up. 'Talking of offices, I have to go now.'

'You'll come back?' Carlton said.

'If you want me to.'

'I most assuredly do, ma'am!' He watched her neat little behind disappear through the door. 'She's nice. Does she belong to anyone?'

'C'mon, Chuck, you're not supposed to talk about women like that anymore. But, as a matter of fact, you're in luck. The lady does not. Belong to anyone, I mean.'

'Well, I guess it's about time my luck started to change.'

'Oh you're lucky, Carlton. You're damned lucky! You're also a celebrity – of sorts. But the fact that your face is in every newspaper, and they're standing in line to have you on every TV chat-show, does not mean that you can play fast and loose with a valued employee of McKenzie Brackman. Understood?'

'Understood. What happened to McIvor?'

'He'll live. Attempted murder – Ron Sharkey defending. I hear the plea may be insanity. Oh, by the way – some unfinished business. I took the liberty, while you're in here, of picking up your mail and taking all messages. This came this morning.' He handed Carlton a long manila envelope franked by the Jupiter Insurance Corporation. It had been opened. Carlton took out the letter and read:

Dear Mr Carlton,

We have endeavoured to contact you several times regarding your latest claim as regards your automobile reg. SY4356 which was involved in a fatal accident on the 18th inst.

Having consulted our files, we must inform you that while you are fully insured against Thirty Party Risk, your current automobile insurance applies only to your Mustang, reg DS55892. I must therefore inform you that since no insurance premium was taken out by yourself regarding your new automobile, this corporation is unable to make any payment towards your claim.

If you have any further queries . . .

'Do I have any *queries*? Look, these people are bandits!'

'No, they're insurance people.'

'But, Mike, that car cost me nearly eighty thousand dollars! You mean they can refuse to pay?'

'They'll try. But I think we've got a case, and we should put up a fight. See you in court!'

'See you in court, Mike. And thanks.'

THE
PARTNERSHIP

CHARLES BUTLER

The same night that Arnie Becker is confined
to a police cell after a drug bust at a yuppie
beach party, Leland McKenzie collapses and is
rushed to hospital. Things couldn't get much
worse for the thriving LA law firm – and then
they do. Without McKenzie present to smooth
things over at MBCK, every minor disaster in
the chain of events that follows combines to
threaten the stability of the partnership.

Price: £3.99
ISBN: 1 85283 601 6

Boxtree will be publishing 2 more LA Law
novels in November 1991.